Secrets of Deltora
Exploring the Land of Dragons

Emily Rodda

Illustrated by Marc McBride

SCHOLASTIC INC.

NEW YORK TORONTO LONDON AUCKLAND SYDNEY
MEXICO CITY NEW DELHI HONG KONG BUENOS AIRES

Note

This centuries-old work by Doran the Dragonlover, Deltora's greatest explorer, was found in a sealed glass case buried beneath some ancient papers in a palace storeroom. The case was marked: "The priceless last work of Withick, Deltora's greatest artist. Do not touch."

Indeed, the book was printed and illustrated by the famous Withick. But it was written by Doran the Dragonlover, on a fateful journey around Deltora during a tumultuous time in our history. The book is part journal, part travel guide. Into it, Doran poured much of his great knowledge of the land he liked to call "The Land of Dragons."

And he did more, as the careful reader will see. Knowing that Prince Gareth, the heir to the throne of Deltora in Doran's time, was to receive the original copy of his book, Doran spoke to Gareth directly, in a way he believed Gareth would understand.

The book has been reproduced exactly, page for page, so that it may be read just as Doran intended.

Conditions in Deltora have changed since Doran's time, but his book is still of great use—not just as a practical guide to travelers and a celebration of Deltora's rich variety, but as a reminder of the need to learn the lessons of history as taught to us by a courageous, ingenious man—a true Deltoran hero.

Lief of Del

Secrets of Deltora

Exploring the Land of Dragons

A Deltoran dragon: protector of the land

Contents

Author's Note

I carried this book with me while I was traveling around Deltora, so some of its pages bear the marks of hard use. I apologize for this. I also apologize for my plain writing style.

I do not need to apologize for the information given within these pages, however. This is a true & complete record of my travels & you can depend upon all the facts & advice given.

I can certainly be justly proud of the printing & paintings, for these are the work of Withick, Deltora's greatest artist, inventor & man of letters.

Before I began my journey, I was given this grand book in which to write my notes. King Lucan himself had sent it to me. He asked that upon my return & when a library copy had been made, the original book should be given to his son & heir, Prince Gareth.

This was a great honor for me—& a pleasure too. Prince Gareth & I rarely see each other now, but when he was a young child he often spent time with me when I was in the palace.

King Lucan's request presented a great problem to the courtiers of Del, however. They knew that my writing would be untidy & my sketches hasty & unpolished—not at all fitting in a book to be presented to the prince. Yet not even the highest official in the palace, Chief Advisor Drumm, would dare to openly disobey a direct order of the king.

Drumm had a solution. He ordered me to write in the king's book only in pencil, so that on my return to the palace a scribe could erase my scrawls & replace them with text in proper form. I was also told that an artist would be appointed to replace my poor sketches with professional illustrations. Then & only then would the book be given to the prince.

As you will see from my Introduction, I agreed to this at the time. I had no choice. It was very likely Gareth would not be able to make sense of my writing in any case. It is nothing like the fine script he is used to. But the longer I was on the road & the more I wrote, the less happy I felt about the plan.

I knew from experience that the palace scribes would change my words & take out any phrases they thought might offend the court. I knew that if I handed the book over to them, there would be a grave danger of my original meaning being lost.

So when I had completed my tour of Deltora, but before I returned to Del, I paid a visit to my friend Withick who now lives in retirement in a peaceful place west of the city.

Withick agreed to help me. Page by page, he did the work the scribes would have done, transforming the book into a work of art. He did it with print created by the amazing machine he had invented & used during his last years in the palace & with pictures produced by his own hand. He changed nothing unless I asked him to—& in truth there were a few small but important alterations to be made to every chapter.

Thanks to Withick, this book is now a valuable & fitting gift for a prince. I have heard that Gareth is no great lover of reading these days, but I pray he will take to heart the important messages that lie within these pages. Even if he never reads the book's full text, I am sure that at least he will be fascinated by the lines of traditional dragon poetry I have used to introduce each chapter. They are unique to this volume. Words will remain to tell the dragons' story, from the end to the beginning, when the dragons & their fire have gone.

Gareth is an intelligent, thoughtful boy—I well remember the word games, codes & other puzzles we enjoyed together in his younger days. Kept closely inside the palace grounds as he is—for his own protection, of course—I am sure he will be interested in learning Deltora's most important secrets through this book's pages.

In faith—

Doran

Explorer in the Time of King Lucan

The Del palace library

1.

Introduction

Fangs, talons, wings
Flame underlined
Are Dragon words.

Traditional Amethyst dragon song

When I was asked to write a book introducing the wonders of Deltora to travelers, my first impulse was to refuse. I am an explorer, not a writer. In addition, I must admit, I had no wish to be chained to a table in the palace library for months while producing a manuscript. Having just returned from a long sea voyage to map Deltora's nearest islands, I was keen to go on the road as soon as possible, to visit the places I had not seen for half a year.

I was then given a personal message from King Lucan. In his note the king explained why he wanted this book to be written & written by me. He said that a practical travelers' guide would not only be of use to Deltora's own citizens, but would also impress & inform our many grand visitors from lands across the seas. My reputation as an explorer, he said, would make readers trust the information the book contained.

King Lucan also said that <u>Prince Gareth</u>, his son,

would benefit from reading about the land he would one day govern. l am sure that this is so, though l believe it would be even better if young Gareth was allowed to travel the realm with me & see it with his own eyes.

Gareth is to be presented with the original copy of the finished book (suitably smoothed & made tidy so as not to offend him). l hope—even pray—that he will learn a little of real life in Deltora by reading my work.

l have been told that l can write while traveling & that l will be given funds to allow me to make a complete tour of the land, so that my information on every area is fresh. l will even have gold enough to buy a horse or obtain other transport should l desire it along the way.

You, reader, may have been able to refuse such an offer, but l found it so tempting that l could not bring myself to refuse it. (As Chief Advisor Drumm, who made the offer, very well knew. No doubt another few months' relief from my vulgar presence & my impertinent remarks about the state of things in Deltora will be very welcome to him.)

So this book will grow as l make my journey. Whatever my doubts, l will complete my task. l can only tell what l know, report what l see & hope it is of use. l have spent my life exploring & mapping Deltora, but even l cannot claim to know all its secrets, let alone to understand them. lt would take several lifetimes to achieve that feat.

As l sit here in the privacy of my usual room in The Seafarer Tavern, filling in the first of these pages, l find l am looking forward to the task ahead. After all, this is the book the king sent me. The king, who these days rarely speaks to anyone except his wife, his son & Chief Advisor Drumm, also sent me a personal message asking for my help! This has convinced me that there is a need for this book—an urgent need. l now have a precious chance to reach many people who might otherwise remain ignorant of Deltora's mysteries.

2.

The Gem Territories

Fiery dashes
After prey.
Fanged words burn.

Traditional Emerald dragon song

Travel in Deltora will be more fruitful & interesting if the traveler is aware of the land's past.

In ancient times, Deltora was known as The Land of Dragons. In my opinion it is a pity that the name was ever changed. The old name was a continual reminder of how closely the dragons are linked to the land they guard & protect.

The land's people were divided into the 7 tribes of Del, Ralad, Plains, Mere, Dread Gnomes, Tora & Jalis. Each tribe had its own territory & each had a powerful talisman, a great gem from beneath its territory's earth.

Legend has it that these gems were the land's gifts to the people following a cataclysmic seaquake that fused their island with a neighboring island & raised the Barrier Mountains in between. The land across the Mountains, once beautiful, is now the Shadowlands. It is ruled by an evil & power-hungry sorcerer called the Shadow Lord.

Tribe	Gem		Symbol of . . .	Powers
Del	Topaz		faith	protects from terrors of the night; opens doors to the spirit world; strengthens & clears the mind; strongest at full moon
Ralad	Ruby		happiness	wards off evil spirits; antidote to snake venom; pales in presence of evil & when misfortune threatens
Plains	Opal		hope	gives glimpses of future; helps the sight; has special affinity with the Lapis Lazuli
Mere	Lapis Lazuli (the heavenly stone)		good fortune	brings luck; has special affinity with the Opal
Dread Gnomes	Emerald		honor	dulls in presence of evil & when a vow is broken; remedy for sores & antidote to poison
Tora	Amethyst		truth	calms & soothes; changes color in presence of illness; fades near poison
Jalis	Diamond		strength & purity	gives courage & strength to worthy wearers; brings misfortune on those who gain it by treachery or for evil purpose

The 7 territories are often known by the names of the tribes that dominated them, for of course people always regard themselves as far more important than the rest of creation! But it is infinitely more practical & appropriate to call them by their gem names, as I do.

The 7 tribes remained separate, jealously guarding their own territories, until the rise of Adin of Del, a blacksmith who was later to become the first king of Deltora. In Adin's time the Shadow Lord had begun a determined invasion, sending monstrous forces into Deltora including a flock of savage giant birds—the 7 Ak-Baba.

These forces were mighty—were sent to destroy.

Dragon attacked by Ak-Baba

The Belt of Deltora

In response to a dream, Adin persuaded each of the 7 tribes to add its talisman to a belt of steel. The magic of the completed dream belt expelled the Shadow Lord's hordes. The tribes united under Adin & the Belt of Deltora, worn* by Adin's heirs, protected the land & strengthened its most ancient defenders—our dragons.

The boundaries of the old tribal territories are now somewhat blurred—for good reason.

Since Adin's time there has been some movement & resettlement, particularly among the people of Del, the Plains & the Mere. Migration from across the sea has also occurred, making changes & offering variety in some areas. The settlement of the people of D'Or in the territory of the Ruby is a shining example of this.

The traveler will still, however, notice distinct differences between the gem territories, notably in the character of the cities & towns, the wildlife, the native people & of course the dragons . . .

*Note: These days the Belt is only actually worn on special occasions. It is usually kept in a glass case at the top of the palace tower.

3.
The Dragons of Deltora

Scales paragraph
Last of dragons' fire.
Word blazing,
Fifth dragon fangs every flame.

Traditional Lapis Lazuli dragon song

Many will tell you that Deltora's dragons—speaking, reasoning beings, wisest & most ancient of all beasts—are nothing but threats to livestock & human life. Such ignorant dolts rejoice as dragon numbers dwindle because of attacks by the monstrous Ak-Baba birds that fly across the mountains from the Shadowlands.

Barring accident or attack, Deltoran dragons can live for 500 years, during which time they continue to grow in size. They tend to be solitary, though enjoying occasional company & they breed only once or twice during their lifetimes. In ancient times the slow breeding rate prevented overpopulation. Today it is a threat to the survival of the species.

Dragon numbers are already dangerously low in all territories. When I was young it was impossible to spend a day in one of Deltora's wild places without seeing a dragon in the sky. Now an adventurer may travel for days without a dragon sighting. I have sent many messages to the king begging him to use the magic of the Belt of Deltora to strengthen the dragons & repel the Ak-Baba, but to date I have received no reply.

I know full well that I have the reputation of being "cracked" on the subject of dragons. But I do not speak for myself alone—I speak on behalf of generations of Deltorans to come. If the earth-wisdom of the dragons vanishes, Deltora will be vulnerable to evil as it has never been in all its long history.

Dragon Watching

Sharp-eyed travelers in Deltora's wild places may still be lucky enough to see & understand one of the most awe-inspiring sights our land has to offer if they refer to the following notes:

❦ There are 7 distinct Deltoran dragon tribes—Topaz, Ruby, Opal, Lapis Lazuli, Emerald, Amethyst & Diamond. Each tribe has its own habits & characteristics. Their territories are strictly defined & correspond exactly to the gem territories of the 7 ancient tribes of the people of Deltora. What more proof should anyone need that in some mysterious way our fortunes & the fortunes of the dragons are linked?

The attached map showing the gem territories is an essential reference for the dragon-watcher. A dragon sighted in, for example, the territory of the Ruby, may be confidently identified as a Ruby dragon even if it is too high for its color to be distinguished. Dragons sense intrusion into their airspace & a dragon that ventures into a rival tribe's territory will be instantly attacked. If possible it will be killed & its teeth scattered.

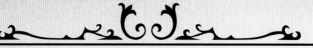

Which Dragon Tribe Is Yours?

People & dragons have existed together in Deltora since ancient times & there is old magic in their relationship.

If fear & prejudice can be put aside, a native Deltoran will feel a strong bond with the dragon tribe that rules in the territory of his or her birth. The Ralad people, for example, feel kinship with Ruby dragons & share many of the Ruby dragons' characteristics. The Dread Gnomes, if they allowed themselves to do so, would see how closely they resemble the dragons of the Emerald, and would admire them & respect them as powerful allies.

The dragons themselves can tell when an individual person was born on their own soil—they can feel it.

I have found that folk who are not Deltoran by birth still find themselves drawn to 1 particular dragon tribe or another. The dragons, too, seem to relate to different foreigners in different ways.

I have come to the conclusion that this is a matter of personality. Each dragon tribe has distinct characteristics. Dragons are drawn to people who resemble them, or particularly admire the characteristics of their gem tribe. People react to dragons in the same way.

If you wish to discover which dragon tribe is yours, consider the characteristics & habits of each tribe as I will describe them when I reach each territory. Make yourself a chart headed with dragon tribe names. Give up to 3 points to each tribe for a characteristic or habit you admire, the number of points depending on how strongly you feel. Take away up to 3 points for a characteristic or habit you do not admire. At the end, the dragon tribe with the highest number of points is probably the tribe with which you have a natural bond. Its territory's gem can then become your own sign & talisman.

Remember, however, that you cannot rely fully on this simple method. If you feel disappointed by the results of your test, because you are strongly drawn to a tribe that did not gain the most points, or if you find that 2 or more tribes score an equal number of points, put your chart aside & choose with your heart. Listen to your instincts. The relationship between people & dragons is mysterious & relies more on the heart than on the head.

Dragons are usually seen on the wing, but you are unlikely to see them if you only glance at the sky occasionally. While the scales of dragons' upper bodies are colored according to their tribe's gem territory, all tribes have pale undersides which change color to blend with the sky in all its moods, providing camouflage when viewed from below. You must find a likely area, then spend time watching the sky for flashes of color as a dragon wheels during hunting or play.

Dragons on the wing

❦ Other large flying creatures such as adult Kin, Ak-Baba
& even eagles are sometimes mistaken for dragons. Note the
color of the flying beast's underside to avoid this error.

❦ Dragons are rarely seen on the ground in these days,
as they keep to rugged places far from human habitation.
The adventurer, however, may still come upon a dragon
unawares, so here are some safety notes:

Dragon Safety Notes

1. Male & female travelers should cover their hair tightly, if the hair is
longer than shoulder length.
2. Dragon lairs are frequently caves or woodland thickets, but some
dragons, notably the Amethyst dragons of the west, sleep in the open.
3. Large caves that are warm & have a sweet, musky smell may be dragon
lairs. It is unwise to enter them.
4. On meeting a dragon by chance, bow your head & stand still. Do not
draw your weapon. Greet the dragon politely, using its gem name (Dragon
of the Ruby, Topaz, etc.). Say you are a traveler, praise the beauty of the
dragon's territory & ask permission to leave its presence.

5. Never turn your back on a dragon.
6. Never ask a dragon its true name. For dragons, knowing an individual's
name is to have power over that individual.
7. Never look into a dragon's eyes. If you do, you may be hypnotized &
perhaps lost.

Dragon Nests

All Deltoran dragon tribes build large, round nests of stones. Nests are lined with soft material, preferably long tresses of human hair, though I have seen nests lined with rabbit skin, sheep fleece, seaweed, dry grass & even, on 1 occasion, a baby's knitted shawl. A single egg is laid in each nest. Twins are very rare, but if they occur they always hatch from the same egg & are identical.

Dragon nest

Eggs of different dragon tribes are colored according to the tribe's scale color. The shells are extremely thick & hard. Eggs do not need to be kept warm. After 6 months, the parents breathe fire upon the egg to encourage hatching. If the parents have died (as is too often the case in these days), another dragon of the same species may choose to breathe on the egg & adopt the emerging young. Unhatched eggs can survive for many years—centuries, I suspect. This could be the dragons' salvation. Various hints & signs have also led me to form the theory that dragons of both genders can, in cases of grave necessity, produce young without a mate.

Newly hatched dragonlings are small enough to fit
in the palm of the hand. They can walk & breathe fire
immediately. They are fed by their parents for 7 days
while their size increases dramatically & their wings grow
strong enough for flight. At a month old they lose their
baby teeth, which are pushed out by the adult fangs that
have formed behind them. Parents encourage dragonlings
to swallow their discarded teeth. Teeth have a mystic
significance for dragons, symbolizing strength, wisdom &
power.

Emerald dragon with dragonling

The nest is abandoned at around this time & the dragonling begins an independent life, though the parents stay near it for up to a year, offering protection & advice.

Note: Never approach a dragon's nest while it is in use. Inspect only abandoned nests, recognized by the following signs.

Signs of nest in use:
Neatly arranged stones, high edges concealing base. Fresh bones & food scraps. Surrounding earth flattened, bare & burned. Strong smell of smoke. Fresh dragon dung. No birds, lizards or other living creatures nearby.

Signs of abandoned nest:
Stones disordered. Edges broken down so base is visible from a distance. Lining material disturbed. Grass, vines, etc., growing around nest. Birds, animals & insects approach nest without fear.

A nesting dragon regards the intruder as a dangerous enemy. It assumes the trespasser plans to do harm, perhaps to injure the young or rob the nest. Dragons of Deltora are vigilant, ferocious guards of their dragonlings. They know their parents are their only protectors.

4.
Deltora's Dangers

> Flames end at wings' promise
> Of fanged sentence flying.
> Each tailtip of dragon word.
> First dragonling!
>
> Opal dragon hatching blessing

While travel in Deltora is always stimulating & rewarding, there is no denying that it can be dangerous for the unwary or ill-informed—& even for the wary & well-informed, on occasion!

My plan is to deal with specific dangers as I reach the places where they may be found. The monster called the Wennbar, for example, will be discussed when I reach the Forests of Silence & the Bubbler when I am in the far north.

While I have been preparing for my journey, however, assembling my usual equipment & supplies, I have realized that travelers from foreign countries who wish to follow in my footsteps may not have the basic knowledge of the land that I, like most other well-traveled Deltorans, take for granted.

Following, therefore, are the dangers that prevail throughout Deltora as a whole.

Dragons

Dragons were discussed in previous pages & there is no need to repeat the information here. Take careful note of the safety precautions I have suggested & follow them to the letter.

Also bear in mind that despite what I have said about usual habitats, dragons are free to fly anywhere within their own territories & can appear in unlikely places—even in towns & cities, though this has lately become very uncommon.

Ak-Baba

As noted earlier, these monstrous, vulture-like birds, known to have helped the sorcerer of the Shadowlands in his battle to conquer Deltora in the time of Adin, are once again patrolling Deltoran skies.

They are usually seen flying in a pack of 7 & careful observation has led me to believe that the pack is always made up of the same 7 birds. I have been called mad for saying so, but it is not beyond belief that these individuals are in fact the very same Ak-Baba that ravaged Adin's army in the final battle against the Shadow Lord's hordes.

We have always called these creatures Ak-Baba because they resemble birds by that name that we know exist in lands across the sea. But the winged monsters that fly from the Shadowlands to attack our dragons are different from the foreign Ak-Baba I have seen in paintings & heard described.

Shadowlands Ak-Baba may well be able to live 1,000 years, as their foreign cousins are said to do, but they are far larger & more ferocious-looking. Unlike true Ak-Baba, they have teeth as well as tearing beaks & they have spines on their backs, necks & heads. They have clearly been bred to fight & kill.

Dangerous spines

Tearing beak

Sharp teeth

Shadowlands Ak-Baba: head detail

Since the time of Adin, there have been no reported Ak-Baba attacks on people or domestic animals. The 7 Ak-Baba are focusing their attention on dragons. Because of this, Deltoran citizens have allowed themselves to be lulled into a false sense of security. Few living in these days would regard Ak-Baba as deserving a place on a list of Deltora's present dangers.

I feel very differently. The beasts are Shadow Lord servants & their orders could change at any time. Reports of Adin's final battle make their willingness to kill & maim ground dwellers perfectly clear. Though they are less than a quarter of an average dragon's size, they are quite powerful enough to snatch an adult human from the ground.

*Ak-Baba: danger to dragon
and human alike*

On Sighting Ak-Baba:

❧ Take cover until the sky is clear.

❧ If there is no cover to be had, flatten yourself on the ground & remain motionless until the Ak-Baba have passed.

❧ If you are attacked, aim knife, spear or arrow at the creature's underside, which is less well protected than the rest of its body. Go for the throat, if you can.

❧ A flaming torch might also be of use. Aim for the eyes & wing feathers.

Bandits, Thieves & Pirates

All lands have their criminals & Deltora is no exception. Though there are certain places where roughnecks are more common—the Barrier Mountains, for example—they can be encountered anywhere.

The problem is not so great that you need to take elaborate measures to protect yourself or your property. Simply travel well armed & avoid attracting unwanted attention by taking the following sensible precautions.

Basic Precautions:

❧ Wear plain, hard-wearing garments, avoiding all finery & jewelry.

❧ Keep most of your gold in a secret pocket or money belt & pay tavern bills, etc., from a small purse in which you keep only enough money for the day.

❧ Avoid grand gestures such as offering to pay for drinks for everyone in a tavern.

❧ Do not boast about your riches or fine possessions within the hearing of strangers.

Barrier Mountains ruffians

Magic

You will encounter magic throughout Deltora—you doubt this at your peril.

I am a practical man. I look for a rational explanation for every event, however mysterious. But since my earliest years I have known that there are things in this ancient land that cannot be explained by reason. Many places are cursed or in some way enchanted. Some individuals have powers beyond the ordinary person's understanding.

In addition, the land itself, its creatures & its plant life, sometimes behave in ways strangers think of as "magical," though they are regarded as quite natural by native Deltorans.

It is important that "magic," whether natural or supernatural, is not taken lightly. It should be treated with the same respect as fire, water or high places, for it has the same power to cause injury to the careless.

Basic Precautions:

❧ Do not injure any part of the land—living or apparently unliving—without good reason. Hunting for food is generally safe, for many beasts in Deltora hunt to survive. Hunting for sport is another matter.

❧ Do not pick & eat any wild fruit, leaf or vegetable without knowing exactly what it is.

❧ Do not jeer at or make fun of unusual-looking persons, or persons who seem to be talking to themselves or to animals, or acting in any other way you find unusual. If someone takes offense at something you have said, apologize politely & quietly move on.

❧ Do not ignore warning notices, especially those beside wells & springs, in front of bridges or at the mouths of caves. Some of these signs are extremely ancient & they are rarely the results of idle superstition.

⤐ Be careful where you light campfires.* In some places they are resented by the earth. If the ground trembles when the fire is lit, put out the fire at once. If a fire goes out more than twice, do not attempt to relight it.

⤐ Sweating, trembling, prickling of the skin, a sudden feeling of intense heat or cold, disturbed vision or an overwhelming feeling of dread may be signs that a place is forbidden to you. If you feel more than 3 of these symptoms at once, obey the warning & turn back.

* Campfires

⤐ It would be impossible for me to list every spot in Deltora where fire is resented by the earth. The safest way to make a fire for warmth or cooking is to benefit from the experience of more seasoned travelers & use 1 of the many fireplaces that I & others have built in suitable camping spots throughout the countryside. These fireplaces are plentiful, except in certain places where fire is unsafe in any case, such as the Shifting Sands in the territory of the Lapis Lazuli, for reasons I will explain later.

⤐ Burn only dead, fallen wood & even then if a stick shows itself to be unwilling, by trembling as you pick it up, by stabbing or scratching you or by dropping from your hand as you carry it, put that stick aside.

⤐ Make sure the fire is out before you leave. This is nothing to do with magic, but is merely practical advice. Any unattended fire can flare up, spread & cause damage.

Equipment & Supplies List

The following items are essential equipment for travelers in Deltora.

map
compass
1 water bottle, to be carried on the belt & refilled at every opportunity
  + 1 extra bottle of water kept for dire emergencies
Travelers' biscuit & dried fruit sufficient for 3 days
1 ball of yellow string
1 metal pot for heating water & cooking
1 strong rope
1 flint or other fire lighter
2 torches
1 all-purpose knife
2 weapons of choice—1 visible, 1 concealed
1 money belt (unless you have a garment with a secret pocket)
1 purse for daily use
1 sleeping blanket
1 pair strong walking boots
2 pairs woolen socks, 1 to be worn, 1 spare
2 sets undergarments, 1 to be worn, 1 spare
1 set strong, plain outer garments
1 sturdy leather belt
1 warm jacket or cloak
1 cap or other secure head covering (if you have long hair)
1 neck scarf for warmth & for covering mouth & nose if necessary
clean bandages kept rolled in a waterproof cloth
healing ointment (I always use Hobson's Salve, available in the Del marketplace)
wax earplugs
snakebite remedy (available in Del marketplace—best buy 2 bottles)
1 pair tweezers for removal of splinters, spines, etc., from skin
1 bar of soap

The following items are not essential, but provide extra comfort:

> 1 oiled sheet (for use as a groundsheet in
> damp places & as a canopy if you are
> forced to sleep outdoors in the rain)
> 1 brush for the teeth
> 1 thin towel
> 1 comb
> 1 bottle Citron to repel insects
> 1 extra set of outer clothing
> 1 pair soft indoor shoes
> herbs for pain relief
> a frying pan
> a tin of tea
> extra food such as dried meat & fish, honey
> & flour for making campfire bread to
> provide variety in the diet between towns
> a simple fishing line + spare hooks & sinkers

My Promise

Drumm, Chief Advisor to King Lucan, has just sent me
a note reminding me to warn intending travelers of how
dangerous Deltora can be. Is he afraid that I will lie
about this? Lying is not my way & in this case it would
be extremely foolish. To make little of our land's dangers
would be to put my readers in peril & this I would
never do. You can trust that all the advice I give will
be accurate. And that I will hide nothing. Lucan himself
could ask no more of me.

5.

Topaz Territory

Heading fire,
Granous under,
Fang note each of talon's word.
First prey.

Topaz dragon feasting song

Topaz Dragons

Color: gold.
Characteristics: reliable, thoughtful, determined, serious, spiritual.
Recent sighting: Os-Mine Hills.
Food: Granous (the gradual increase in the numbers of these vicious denizens of the Os-Mine Hills is a direct result of the drop in Topaz dragon numbers), Vine-weaver Birds, Dragon Lizards, fish, domestic animals (rarely).

It is fitting that my tour will begin in the land of the Topaz because this territory's great city, Del, is the first point of call for most visitors to Deltora's shores.

This is not to say that I believe, as too many palace courtiers do, that Del is supremely important & the hub around which the rest of Deltora revolves! Most of those exquisitely clad fops have never set foot outside their city's walls. They know little of the rest of their own territory & nothing at all about the wonders of Deltora as a whole.

Foreigners are attracted to Del because it is the largest Deltoran center. Also because its broad, calm harbor provides a safe refuge for the ships of traders, adventurers & grand folk alike & the city's inhabitants are used to doing business with strangers. In addition, of course, Del is the home of the king, who unlike his royal ancestors rarely travels outside his city, preferring to invite noble foreigners & important Deltorans to his palace.

Topaz territory, of course, is far more than Del. Its coastline & countryside are delightful to explore.

The River of Del is clear, swift flowing & full of fish. The Os-Mine Hills are famous for their beauty & healthful air. Most visitors to Del also soon hear of the Forests of Silence, but I will leave them out of this chapter. As they present particular problems & lie across the borders of Ruby & Topaz territories, I will give them a chapter of their own.

The Palace

The palace stands on a hill in the center of Del & is visible from every part of the city. It must be an object of curiosity to travelers—even those, like myself, who prefer fresh air & open spaces to piles of stone, however elegantly arranged.

My personal knowledge of the palace is limited (since I loathe the place & spend as little time in it as possible). The palace librarians have kindly provided me with the following facts & figures.

The palace of Del

✦ In common with every other important Deltoran building since the time of Adin, the palace was designed & made by the builders of Raladin. It took 40 years to complete. It is considered by many—especially those who live in it—to be a triumphant expression of Deltora's greatness & power.

✦ The palace was built by order of King Brandon, the father of Lucan, our present king. As soon as the ground floor was finished King Brandon went into residence, leaving the blacksmith's forge, which had been the traditional home of the heirs of Adin since the defeat of the Shadow Lord & the uniting of the 7 tribes.

✦ The palace is built of local sandstone & roofed with slate. The floors & internal pillars are of marble.

✦ The ceilings in the formal rooms are lavishly decorated with painted scenes of Deltora's past, the ceilings of the Great Hall & Banqueting Hall featuring borders of pure gold. The paintings were created by Withick, Deltora's greatest artist & inventor. The library ceiling is particularly fine. It depicts Opal dragons swooping from the sky to fight with Adin's army against the Shadow Lord's hordes on the Hira plain. Some people (Chief Advisor Drumm, for example) think it too savage for a library, but it is much admired by visitors.

✦ The palace has 3 main floors & a high tower in which the Belt of Deltora is kept for safety (though many people, including myself, would feel far safer if the Belt was kept around the

The palace library

king's waist where it belongs). A chapel & a series of cellars—the latter all too easily suited to conversion into dungeons, I fear—lie below ground level.

✦ It has the amazing total of 200 rooms (if you count the storerooms, pantries & lavatories!), including 25 guest bedrooms, a banqueting hall where 250 guests can feast, the Great Hall, which can accommodate 1,000 people, a magnificent library spacious enough to store 100,000 books & a large, warm & friendly kitchen (which I infinitely prefer to all of the above).

The City of Del

Del is a busy, crowded city, where every kind of shop,
stall & industry may be found. Strolling along its winding
streets the traveler will see many strange sights & hear
many languages spoken. Most people are friendly &
helpful to strangers, especially strangers who have a little
money to spend.

Inns abound throughout the city. I recommend The
Topaz, The King's Arms & The Golden Dragon for those
willing to pay a good price for a bed. The People's Palace,
The Vine-Weaver, The Seafarer & The Blue Jug offer the
cleanest rooms for folk of lesser means.

While preparing for my journey I have spent some
hours each day wandering through the city trying to see it
with the fresh eyes of a visitor. Crowded cities are not to
my taste & I rejoice that I will be leaving here tomorrow,
but I know that this book would not be considered
complete without some information on Del's attractions, so
I list them below.

Places of Special Interest

The library contains much of interest

❦ **The palace.**
Visitors may
tour some
of the great
rooms if a
palace guard
is available to
guide them. It
is wise to make
an appointment
the day before.
Visitors
who are not
neatly dressed
will not be

admitted. The library on the 3rd floor is open to members of the public each afternoon. The palace librarians will supervise your visit. They will bring you any books you require. It is, however, permitted to browse the shelves alone & I suggest you do this. Who knows what forgotten treasure you may find hidden in a dusty corner?

❧ **The dock area.** Much trade is conducted here & exotic goods are unloaded for sale in the city & beyond. Hot drinks, cheese pastries, sausages, spicy rice balls & baked potatoes are readily available from the street sellers who throng the area. The taverns are colorful, but can be rowdy & are perhaps unsuitable for folk of elegant manners. They do, however, offer cheap ale & excellent company for those of us who care more for good hearts than for good manners.

❧ **The market square.** The market is in the city's center. Here it is possible to hear every Del rumor & buy everything from a humble corn cake to a Fighting Spider from the Plains or an intricate puzzle-box from across the Ocean of the South. The square is easy to find—all Del's roads seem to lead to it. The crowds are always dense & you should beware of pickpockets.

❧ **The sandy shores on either side of the dock area.** These shores are still unspoiled & provide stunning views of the Ocean of the South. The traveler who does not care for swimming can hire a small boat, or simply watch the fishing craft that throng the area.

❧ **The pottery of Piper's Lane.** This pottery is famous throughout Deltora for the excellence of its wares & the deep blue glaze that is its trademark. The Del Pottery is a family business & has been so since before the rise of Adin.

❧ **The River Tor.** The Tor runs down to the sea on the western edge of Del. The riverbanks are shaded by trees &

Beware of unsavory characters in the market square

smothered with sweet-smelling violets in the spring. If you
wish to escape from city smells & bustle for a time, you
will find refuge beside the Tor.

❧ **Adin's forge.** The home of the great Adin & his heirs
till King Brandon's time is still a working blacksmith's
forge. It is now privately owned & is not open to tourists.
It is no longer even marked, since the present blacksmith
objected to the constant interruptions caused by visitors
eager to pay homage to the place where the Belt of
Deltora was forged.

No one could object, however, to a visitor merely
looking at the forge from the outside. It stands about 5
minutes' brisk walk toward the shore from the bottom of
the palace hill.

Main Roads from Del

The Coast Road hugs the length of the Topaz shoreline, continuing east into Ruby territory & west into the territory of the Diamond. The road is narrow but smooth & safe. It provides an excellent way of seeing some of the country, particularly for those who prefer riding to walking. Whales, sea serpents & dragons hunting fish may be sighted along the way. The road provides glorious views & the notorious Forests of Silence may be safely observed from parts of it.

    The Great North Road is the road most often taken by those who wish to travel directly to the heart of Ruby territory, or to visit the Forests of Silence or the Os-Mine Hills. It is always kept in excellent repair because it leads to the farming areas of the north & northeast* & is used by farmers to bring produce into the city for sale.

    ***Note:** These areas are seldom visited by tourists, yet the countryside is very beautiful & the low, rolling hills & plains make for very easy walking. The villages are old & entirely unspoiled. People are typically friendly & at almost every farmhouse the well-mannered traveler can always be sure of a good meal & a bed (if only a pile of straw in a barn) in return for a few silver coins or a couple of hours' work.

    Deltora Way runs west through the territory of the Diamond, Opal & Lapis Lazuli to the city of Tora in the territory of the Amethyst. This road was built by order of the great Adin, who was eager to forge strong links between the 2 cities. It has been a little neglected of late & bandits can be troublesome in its more deserted parts, but it is still the shortest & best track for those wishing to travel directly to the northwest.

    There. I believe I have now written enough about Del & can leave for the Os-Mine Hills tomorrow with a clear conscience. In truth, I would have left anyway, clear conscience or no. I have had more than enough of the city & long for fresh air & open spaces.

The Os-Mine Hills

I am writing to you now high in the Os-Mine Hills. The sun is sinking low in the sky. The air is cool & sweet & full of birdcalls. A Topaz dragon is flying high above me, stretching his wings after spending an hour in conversation with me on my hilltop. It is good to be here, but my heart is heavy.

I was glad to find the dragon alive & well & told him so. He answered soberly that others of his tribe have not been so fortunate. Very many have been slaughtered by the Ak-Baba over the past few months. In fact, my friend is starting to fear that few Topaz dragons now survive, for he has not seen a single member of his tribe since the last full moon.

This is grave news indeed. I can hardly believe that so much damage has been done in the short time since I was here last. It is as if the Ak-Baba, after years of occasional raids, are now waging deliberate & full-scale war on Deltora's dragons—in Topaz territory, at least.

Not a word of this has reached Del. It is tempting to go back at once & insist on seeing King Lucan—storm his chamber, if necessary. But this would be folly & I know it. Any attempt to force my way into King Lucan's presence would certainly fail & add to my reputation of being unhinged. Besides, Chief Advisor Drumm hates me as it is. He would enjoy seeing me disgraced. I would be playing right into his hands if I returned to Del now, abandoning the task the king has set me.

No doubt I should erase the last paragraph—but let it stand. I will leave it to the person who copies these notes to delete it. It relieves my feelings to see it there for now.

Until the dragon returns, I will occupy my time usefully by writing my notes about the Os-Mine Hills. I had planned to stay here for several days & then spend some leisurely weeks touring the farming areas of the northeast. But now I feel I must move on to the Forests of Silence as soon as I am able. There are always dragons there. I need to know how many.

So . . . the Os-Mine Hills . . .

The Os-Mine Hills are 3 days' walk or just over a day's ride to Del's north, almost on the border of Ruby territory. They can be reached by taking the Great North Road from Del and turning left at the Os-Mine signpost, or by simply following the River Del upstream. This is a more attractive path, in my opinion & the way I myself have chosen to take.

The Hills are well worth visiting for their rugged beauty & the unique bird, plant & animal life to be found in their forests. In the past they were also ideal for dragon watching, as they were favorite haunts of Topaz dragons.

The vicious creatures known as Granous,* once rarely seen above ground, are now becoming something of a problem, but there are not so many that the hills should be avoided.

*Granous

❧ Only found in the Os-Mine Hills, Granous are cunning, bloodthirsty beings that live & hunt in packs of 6–10.

❧ One Granous is very like another. They are generally not much taller than a Dread Gnome, but are much bulkier & covered in matted gray hair. They are horribly like humans, because they walk upright & can speak & reason, even enjoying games of skill, but there the resemblance ends.

❧ Dragon prey as they are, Granous typically live in underground dens.

❧ Now the Hills are full of their tunnels. They tend to use these tunnels to follow & watch victims for some time, waiting for a moment's inattention or weakness, such as a fall, before launching an attack.

❧ Surviving as they normally do on Vine-weaver Birds, wood mice, rock rats, snakes & young dragon lizards, Granous relish human & horse flesh.

❧ In addition to a good weapon prominently displayed, a show of strength & confidence will usually keep Granous off at first. They are basically cowardly. But after some time watching you, they will become frustrated & unpredictable.

❧ Each day that passes your danger increases, so it is wise to stay alert. Once Granous make up their minds to attack, they are ruthless enemies & some pack leaders are more aggressive than others.

❧ Territory locals will tell you that if Granous capture you they will not kill you at once. Instead they will toy with you, asking you trick questions & biting off a finger or toe for every wrong answer. This is why a concealed weapon is a sensible precaution for every Os-Mine traveler.

Granous

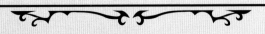

Safety Precautions

❦ It is best not to go into the Hills alone. The terrain can be rough & there is always the danger of accident or Granous attack.

❦ Every member of the party should carry 2 weapons—1 clearly visible & 1 concealed.

❦ Wear sturdy boots & take warm clothing, including hat & gloves. The Hills can become very cold at night.

❦ It is safest to lead horses rather than to ride through the Hills, to avoid the danger of being thrown when the horse startles or stumbles, as it surely will at some time or another during the journey.

❦ Carry your own food & at least some water. There are many springs & clear streams, but there is always the chance that your party will be besieged by Granous in a place where water is not available. Food suitable to humans is scarce. Do not eat any fruits or berries that you have not seen birds eat first. Do not attempt to eat Granous flesh. It is full of parasites & will make you violently ill.

❦ Sleep in shifts to avoid surprise Granous attack.

❦ Follow general dragon safety precautions as described.

Sights of Special Interest

❦ **Topaz dragons.** Watch for them on hilltops, or in the sky when birds give warning cries & scatter.

❦ **Vine-weaver birds.** These birds are unique to the Os-Mine Hills. They use their long, narrow beaks to make intricate net-like nests in which they live all year round.

The nests are usually high, but can easily be seen lacing the tops of the trees. Vine-weavers themselves are small, gray & undistinguished, but it is fascinating to watch the skill with which they weave & knot the vines, constantly repairing, thickening & enlarging their nets. They live in large flocks & the air of the Hills rings with their whistling, particularly at dawn.

❦ **Dragon lizards.** These lizards are found among the rocks of the foothills & also in valley caves at higher levels. Since they are gold in color & as large as a calf, excluding the tail, they are sometimes mistaken for dragon young, but are in fact a totally different species (as any fool with half an eye can see). They have no wings, cannot breathe fire & eat only insects, birds & small snakes. They will bite & scratch humans if threatened, but if left alone they are harmless.

Dragon lizard—in no way related to the real thing

They are becoming rare, as they are frequently killed by the fearful & their gold-colored eggs are often taken from their pebble nests as souvenirs or for sale as "dragons' eggs." Since dragon lizard eggs are no larger than duck eggs, it is difficult to understand how anyone could believe they belong to true dragons, but people are gullible, it seems.

❖ **Butter moths.** These insects are worth mentioning because they are so numerous in the Hills' thickly forested valleys. They are bright yellow & can be as large as a man's hand from wing tip to wing tip. Their caterpillars hang in squirming bundles from bushes & the lowest branches of trees & are relished by dragon lizards.

I see my dragon friend is returning to me, so I will put my book & pencil away for now. There is a lot more that could be said about the Os-Mine Hills, of course, but I believe I have covered the main points. Later I will eat & sleep. No Granous will approach me while the dragon is near.

At dawn I will set out for the Forests of Silence.

6.

The Forests of Silence

Dragon marks question
Wings after words.

Traditional Ruby dragon lament

I reached the Forests of Silence 3 days ago but I still have not seen a single dragon. Never before has this happened. It makes me very uneasy. The forest beasts usually hunted by the dragons are more numerous. Clearly what I began to suspect in the Os-Mine Hills is true—dragon numbers dropped dramatically while I was away on my sea voyage.

I have neglected this journal during my time here. My mind has been on other things, but this is no excuse. Tonight I will make up for lost time. It is not easy to write high in a tree, but I have a lantern for light & I do not feel like sleep in any case.

The 3 linked woods to the northeast of Del have an evil reputation that is well deserved. Most visitors to Del soon hear tales of their dangers & naturally the more adventurous soon become wild to see the Forests of Silence for themselves.

I have given the Forests a separate section because most of the information & advice I can provide applies to all of them, yet they bridge territory borders (see foldout map). First Wood lies solely in Topaz territory, but part of Mid Wood & the whole of Last Wood (more commonly called End Wood these days) are in the territory of the Ruby.

Note: The Forests of Silence are not recommended for the inexperienced, unarmed or fearful traveler or anyone weakened by age or infirmity.

Nevertheless, there are few more beautiful or fascinating places in Deltora, and the watchful adventurer can avoid the worst of the dangers by following a few simple precautions.

Safety in the Forests

◆ Enter the Forests only in full daylight. Leave yourself enough time to be well out of the trees before sunset.

◆ Do not go alone. Take at least 1 companion, preferably more. It is true that I have traveled through the Forests alone on many occasions, but it would be irresponsible for me to encourage others to follow my example.

◆ Mark your track to avoid becoming lost. A good method is to use lengths of yellow string tied firmly to bushes & trees. Be sure to remove the strings on your return journey, so as not to confuse other travelers.

Note: It is not advisable to mark the trees in any permanent way, as they are likely to take offense & some will attempt to wreak revenge by such means as dropping branches or snakes on your head, and hurling down vine loops to trip or strangle you.

◆ If by misfortune you find yourself overtaken by sunset, climb a tree that appears friendly* and remain on a high branch till dawn. One member of the party should be awake & on guard at all times. Do not return to the ground until the patches of sunlight on the forest floor are larger than your hand with fingers spread.

Some trees will take revenge if injured

*How to Tell if a Tree Is Friendly

❧ Press the palms of your hands firmly against the trunk. If the tree is friendly you will feel nothing. If it is unfriendly you will feel a faint, buzzing vibration as if the trunk is full of angry bees.

❧ Unfriendly trees dislike human contact & will resist being climbed. Even friendly trees occasionally wish to be left in peace. If you lose your footing more than 3 times while attempting to climb a tree, it is safest to leave that tree & try another.

❦ Carry food and water with you. Many of the fruits of the Forests are edible—even delicious—but many others are poisonous, have odd effects (such as severe itching, numbness in the mouth & tongue, permanent staining of lips & hands giving a "tattoo" effect, etc.) or are jealously guarded by dangerous beasts. It is unwise for the stranger to experiment. The stream that runs through all 3 Forests, finally discharging into the River Del, is pure, but it is not always possible to reach it without danger, so it cannot be counted upon.

❦ Be alert at all times. The dangers you may encounter are too numerous to list fully, but I have mentioned some of the most common in the notes that follow.

Dangers Common to All Woods

Snakes, swamps, poisonous fungi, biting lizards, wild cats & so on will surely be expected by the traveler brave (or foolish) enough to defy all warnings & enter any of the woods.

I have confined myself, therefore, to listing 4 dangers that are common in the Forests but are found nowhere else, so may be unfamiliar to the traveler.

Silence Spiders

Extremely venomous spiders, black with a red stripe. They are not particularly large—the biggest I have seen was no broader than my index finger—but what they lack in size they make up in aggression. Unlike most spiders, a Silence Spider will actually attack an intruder who ventures too close to its web, leaping outward with enormous speed, trailing a thread of silk behind it & generally aiming for the head. A bite from a Silence Spider is almost instantly fatal, which gives a grim double meaning to its name.

Silence Spider

Sunrays

These are large yellow carnivorous plants that grow at
ground level in shady areas. The long, fleshy leaves, which
can be as long as a man is tall, fan out from a center that
resembles a pile of red berries & lie flat to the ground,
forming an almost perfect circle easily mistaken for a patch
of sunlight. Anything living that unwarily walks upon the
Sunray is quickly trapped & devoured as the leaves snap
shut with astonishing speed, furling to form a thick spear.

　　Usual prey: Wenn, birds, snakes, wood mice & Leaf
Creepers, but larger specimens can and do trap & digest
average-sized humans.

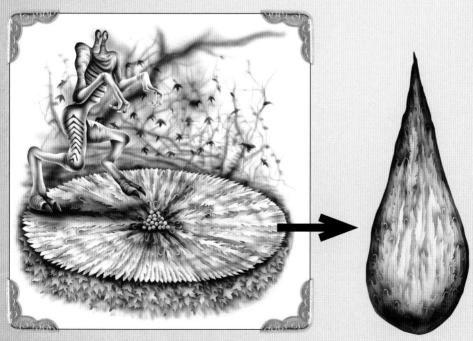

An unwary Wenn steps into a Sunray and is devoured

Coffin Pods

Woody pods that hang from the flowering branches of the Coffin Tree. The red, orchid-like blooms of the tree are beautiful, but the pods are vicious, and snap at any living thing that passes. They can kill insects, lizards & small birds, but are not large enough to do humans more harm than severing an ear or a finger. Nevertheless they should be avoided, particularly in First Wood, since the smell of warm blood is attractive to the Wennbar.

Flesh Pythons

Flesh Pythons are so called because of their glistening red, apparently skinless appearance. Most are about the length of a large eel, but I have seen specimens twice or even 3 times that size. They have no fangs, but kill

Flesh Pythons

their prey (any living creature they can take unawares, including members of their own species) by strangling & swallowing whole. They are ground-dwelling & usually sleep coiled in fern beds during the day, coming out in great numbers to hunt by night. Fortunately they cannot climb trees.

Commonly Asked Questions

Are Flesh Pythons really skinless? I assure you they are not. They exude a slime that creates this impression.

Do Sunrays make a sound? Will make a purring sound when fully fed.

How can I make a Sunray release someone? Persuade it to open by burning it with a lighted torch.

Which of the Forests is the safest? Last or End Wood, the Forest farthest from Del.

Do Flesh Pythons have predators? Dragons, the Wennbar & members of their own species.

How can I avoid being bitten by a Silence Spider? To avoid Silence Spiders, watch for webs strung between 2 trees.

How can I protect myself from Flesh Pythons at night? Sleep in a tree.

Will Flesh Python numbers keep increasing? Until Topaz dragon numbers rise again, they will.

Is it always dark in the Forests? Skies are hidden by the trees, so the Forests are usually dim, even on fine days.

Do Coffin Pods know if they are attacking humans or beasts? Become a Coffin Pod & you will know. I cannot tell you.

Why are dangerous places like the Forests of Silence allowed to exist? Safe places for humans exist in great numbers all over Deltora. The Forest plants & beasts only have 1 home. It is not their fault if you choose to enter their domain.

I long to see the Forests, but I am afraid. What should I do? Again, I cannot tell you. You must weigh the evidence & decide for yourself.

First Wood

✦ This is the Forest closest to Del, so it is the Forest most often visited or stumbled upon by strangers. Local people generally keep well away from it. It is the largest of the 3 Forests & contains a huge variety of unusual plant & animal life.

✦ The only safe path to First Wood is Num's Way, which branches off the Great North Road to the right, about 4 hours' brisk walk from Del. Do NOT attempt to use the shortcut through Wenn Del, which you will reach earlier (see map). This path is infested by dangerous creatures called Wenn (see below).

I have seen to it that the Wenn Del path is clearly marked with a warning sign. I have also tried to block the path, but the Wenn undo my work the moment my back is turned. Once I destroyed the bridge that is part of the path. It was rebuilt overnight.

Dangers Unique to First Wood

✦ **Wenn.** Pale, cold-blooded, stinging creatures about the height of an average 10-year-old child. Wenn paralyze

Wenn

their victims—not in order to eat them, for Wenn eat
only the leaves of certain bushes—but to offer them
as sacrifices to their god, a monstrous beast called the
Wennbar (see below).

Red eyes in the bushes & a high-pitched humming
sound are signals of Wenn presence. Do not attempt
to stand & fight. Wenn hunt in packs & the humming
sound is disabling. Put in your earplugs immediately (see
equipment list) & climb the nearest tree. Wenn cannot
climb & after an hour or so they will grow tired of
waiting & disperse to search for other prey.

❧ **The Wennbar.** A huge, noxious reptile that relishes
warm flesh. It sees the whole of First Wood as its
territory & is extremely savage. It usually emerges from
its den only at sunset, but has been known to prowl in the
hours of daylight, particularly on overcast or rainy days.
It appears slow-moving, but do not be deceived. When
roused, it can move with astonishing speed.

A tree is the only safe refuge from the Wennbar, but
do not remain on a low branch. The monster's neck can
extend like a telescope, enabling it to reach far higher than
you would think. I have seen it snatch birds from the air.

The Wennbar

Mid Wood

The central and smallest of the 3 Forests, Mid Wood straddles the border between the Topaz & Ruby territories. It is notable for its varied birdlife & small, furred beasts such as squirrels, wood mice & tiny, bright-eyed, highly intelligent creatures called Siskis, which are sadly becoming rare due to the rapid increase in Flesh Python numbers.

Mid Wood is most easily entered by turning right off the Great North Road into a narrow track called Knight's Bane Lane. If you do decide you must see the Wood for yourself, keep very close to the edge—15 minutes' walk from the first line of trees will enable you to see all the variety Mid Wood has to offer. Do not, under any circumstances, allow any member of your party to go farther. Avoid the center.

Danger Unique to Mid Wood

- **The Dark.** A small, spider-webbed, vine-hung clearing in the Forest's center is known to local people as "The Dark." It is rumored that the ghost of a Jalis knight called Gorl guards The Dark. You may be told that these rumors are merely the result of ignorant superstition springing from an ancient folktale. This is not true. There is a malignant, gold-armored presence in the center of Mid Wood—I have seen it for myself & narrowly escaped with my life.

It is said that Gorl guards the fabled Lilies of Life,

The formidable Gorl—by no means seek him out

having killed both his brothers in a quarrel over the Lilies' life-giving nectar in the time before the uniting of the 7 tribes. I do not know if this is true. I saw no flowers, fabled or otherwise, in that grim place. Gorl challenged me at the entrance of his enclosure & I made haste to flee as he suggested before his sword could sever my head from my body.

It is my opinion, however, that no flower could bloom in the darkness Gorl has created by encouraging vines to roof his enclosure, so if the Lilies do exist, their miraculous nectar remains locked within them—and will do so until Gorl falls to dust at last & the vines are removed to let in the sun.

If this information stimulates your curiosity—even encourages you to seek out The Dark & pit yourself against Gorl—I beg you to use the sense the Maker gave you & put such thoughts aside. Gorl has supernatural strength & the power to bend others to his will. No weapon can prevail against him. Rumor has it that every soul who has attempted to fight him has died in the attempt & I believe this to be true. Looking past him into the murk of his enclosure, I could see no flowers, but on the ground I could clearly see the gleam of human bones.

Last or End Wood

End Wood is where I am now. It lies fully in Ruby territory. To reach it, turn right off the Great North Road at the Ringle crossroad.

In my opinion End Wood is the least dangerous of all the Forests of Silence, and the most pleasurable to visit, as long as the usual precautions are taken. The ferns are particularly varied & unusual & the atmosphere is less oppressive than that of the other Forests, perhaps because the trees are more widely spaced. It makes a good shortcut to the town of Broome on Deltora's east coast.

Dangers Unique to End Wood

❧ **Orchard Keepers.** If you come upon a tempting grove of fruit trees growing in shallow water, turn away from it. The fruit should not be eaten unless its hard, bitter skin is eaten also. Folk who eat the flesh of the fruit alone will quickly fall into a drugged sleep & become the prey of a giant, carnivorous waterbird called the Orchard Keeper.

    I have seen 2 Orchard Keeper groves in End Wood. There could easily be more.

❧ **Land Limpets.** These are hard-shelled creatures no larger than my thumbnail. They occur in large numbers in some End Wood fern beds & attach themselves to the exposed flesh of any living creature that passes. They do not appear to suck blood, or indeed do any damage to their host while they are attached, but when they are removed (which can only be done by the application of a hot iron to their shells) they leave a red patch which very quickly becomes an ulcer. Land Limpet ulcers can take months to heal & always result in a deep pockmark that many people find upsetting, particularly if it is upon the face.

———◆———

I managed to sleep a little after finishing my notes. I am now waiting for the sun to rise. When its rays fall on the Forest floor it will be safe to climb down to the ground & leave here. I have decided to go straight to the town of Ringle, which is not far away from End Wood.

7.

Ruby Territory

Burning symbol,
Ralad fire.
Third dragon flies,
Every scale blazing.

Ruby dragon sunrise chant

The territory of the Ruby, the ancient home of the Ralad tribe, is generally more rugged & wild than the land of the Topaz & teems with animal & bird life. It does not lack people, however. There are 3 main towns— Broome, Raladin & D'Or (which is more a city than a town, in truth) & many farms, smaller towns & villages where the traveler can rest & obtain fresh supplies.

Ringle—A Good Place to Rest

The first stopping place for most visitors to the territory of the Ruby is the thriving market town of Ringle, reached by turning left at the well-marked crossroad on the Great North Road.

Ringle is a good place to spend a couple of nights. There is a small public bathhouse, which also provides tubs for the washing of clothes. In the market in the town center you will find a wide variety of foods,

Ruby Dragons

Color: rich red sometimes deepening to maroon.
Characteristics: kind, good-natured, slow to anger, good sense of humor, enjoy games.
Recent sighting: Broome coast, Dragon's Nest.
Food: fish, Pig Rats, snakes, Painted Plain Deer.

both fresh & dried, to replenish your supplies.

Ringle has only 2 inns—The Ringle Rest & The Jolly Goat—but many of the townsfolk have spare bedrooms they are willing to let to travelers of respectable appearance. These rooms vary in price & quality & are advertised by notices pinned to a board in the town center. In addition, most of the neighboring farmers will allow a traveler to camp in their fields in return for an hour's work chopping wood or forking hay. Some of these fields have small fireplaces & all have a pump, a well or a stream supplying fresh water.

As I am presently in funds & in any case have work to do (for I am determined to keep this book up-to-date), I am presently luxuriating by the fire in the guest parlor of The Jolly Goat. I am quite private here—the other guests have joined the locals in the bar where a darts competition is taking place. My roast chicken dinner was very good & The Jolly Goat's ale is excellent. The sound of rain pelting down outside makes my present comfort even more enjoyable.

But my eyelids have begun to droop & early on the morrow I will be setting out for 1 of the few large towns in Deltora that I always thoroughly enjoy visiting—Broome. A few words on this subject follow before I retire for the night.

Traveling to Broome

Broome lies on a wild & beautiful stretch of land on Deltora's east coast, almost completely hemmed in by the Barrier Mountains, End Wood & the sea.

Because it is so isolated, travelers are often tempted to forget Broome & move straight on from Ringle to the city of D'Or. This is understandable & perhaps wise for those who find noise & rough manners offensive & take no pleasure in wild scenery.

For the true adventurer, however, the Broome area

should not be missed. It is a unique part of Deltora & besides offers an excellent chance of seeing at least 1 Ruby dragon.

    Note: It is traditional for every unexpected visitor to Broome to present a gift of food to the town. Your gift can be as small as a bunch of wild celery or as large as a box of toffee sweets or a clutch of partridge eggs. It is the token that is important.

    The shortest way to Broome from Ringle is through End Wood & across the Painted Plain, so called because of its rich carpet of grass & wildflowers. The Plain is a good source of wild food* & is much visited by Broome hunters. This route is not recommended to the inexperienced. A longer but safer route is to skirt End Wood & travel south along the last part of the Mountain Road, which runs beside the Barrier Mountains.

    Either way you will eventually reach the Capricon Hills, a range of low hills beyond which are Broome & the sea.

*Foods of the Painted Plain

❧ **Pig Rats.** These are plump, furred beasts that can grow to the size of a large hare. They are very tasty roasted or stewed with parsley, wild celery & onion. Favorite prey of the Ruby dragons & with no other predators but humans, Pig Rats have lately increased vastly in number. They are ground-dwelling, feed mainly on grass & lily roots & are best hunted with arrows or spears as they are wily & difficult to trap.

❧ **Nodnaps.** These are fleshy, gray, ground-dwelling birds about the size of a half-grown hen. They run in preference to flying, graze the Plain in flocks of up to 100 & are easily caught. They taste a little like turkey when roasted. Beware of small bones.

❧ **Wild herbs.** Celery, mint, fennel, parsley & thyme.

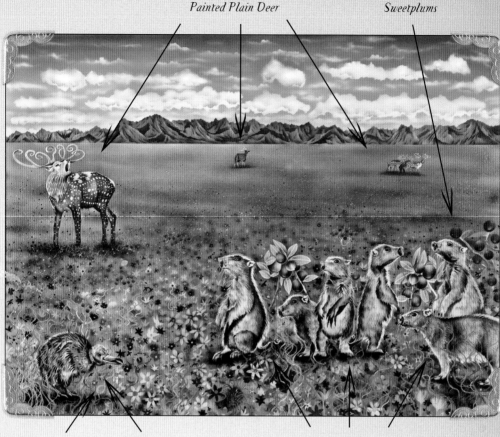

Painted Plain Deer   Sweetplums

Traveler's Weed   Nodnap   Pig Rats

❦ **Traveler's Weed.** This is a clump-like plant with curly bright green leaves that have a refreshing, slightly peppery taste when eaten raw. Traveler's Weed is not unique to the Painted Plain, but is very common throughout Ruby territory. I urge you to try it. It is an excellent way of obtaining fresh green vegetable when nothing else is available & is held to be very good for the digestion.

❦ **Sweetplums.** These delicious round purple fruits have a distinctive rich perfume. They are borne on low bushes that tend to grow in clumps. They can be found throughout Ruby territory & are highly recommended.

    Note: On the plain you will also see **Painted Plain Deer**—medium-sized deer, spotted tan & white, with spiraling white horns. In my opinion the deer are not suitable food for travelers & are best left to the Broome hunters, the dragons & themselves. These deer are far too large for 1 beast to be consumed by a single party of travelers in the time it takes to cross the plain.

    I am not sentimental, but dislike hunting that involves waste.

The Town of Broome

Broome is a walled town of square white towers & sturdy buildings. Its energetic people are of every color, shape & size. They are mostly the descendants of castaways once marooned on this wild shore—shipwrecked sailors & pirates, mutineers, escaping slaves & stowaways thrown overboard to swim or drown.

They are fisherfolk, farmers & hunters now, but the hot blood of adventurers & risk-takers burns in their veins. They make generous hosts & loyal friends, but are quick to take offense at any suspected insult or slight. For this reason, be sure to take note of the following advice.

First Entry to the Town

❧ As you walk toward the town gate, lift your hands, palms forward, to shoulder height.

❧ When the guard challenges you, stop & state your name clearly. The guard will then ask you to step forward. This is the signal for you to lower your hands.

❧ At the gate, offer the gift of food you have brought for the town. Whatever its value, apologize for its smallness.

❧ The guard will take the gift, welcome you, direct you to the nearest guesthouse & stand aside to let you pass.

❧ Thereafter you can enter & leave the town at will.

Broome Manners

❧ It is considered rude to stare at others in the street, or to comment, even flatteringly, on anyone's appearance. You may find this difficult at first—much Broome clothing looks very colorful to strangers & many of the women have shaved heads painted in exotic patterns (a traditional protection against dragon attack).

A woman of Broome

❧ Always return any greeting, or risk a rough challenge to fight.

❧ It is considered the height of bad manners to refuse an invitation to dance, unless you are visibly injured or a known invalid.

❧ Never complain about your accommodation or the food you are given to eat. If you do, you will be firmly asked to leave, whatever the time or the weather.

❧ It is a Broome custom to remain within the city during the hour of sunset.

Capricons

In the hills around Broome you may see, or even meet, blue-eyed slender beings whose bodies look human from the waist up, but goat-like from the waist down. These are Capricons, the original inhabitants of the ancient city of Capra, which once stood where Broome stands today.

Capra is said to have been the most beautiful city of ancient times. It was destroyed before the time of Adin by Ruby dragons angered because the Capricons would not stop killing the dragons' young. It was at that time that

Capricons looking down on Broome

the Capricons retreated to the hills. Much later, Broome was built on Capra's ruins. The Capricons hate & resent the new city & will not go near it.

Capricon Precautions

❧ If you meet a Capricon, it is best to bow politely & move on without speaking. Capricons loathe all who are not their kin. If you greet one, he or she will certainly answer with rage & disgust & may spit at you or even throw stones.

❦ If you find dishes of bread, fruit & vegetables lying about outside the city walls, do not touch them. The food is left out nightly by people in Broome for the Capricons, who otherwise would have little to eat, for they do not hunt or farm. The Capricons sneer at the food & at those who leave it for them, but they depend on it for their lives.

❦ Capricons are most often seen at sunset, gathered on a hilltop & staring down at Broome. It is said that they are looking at a vision of Capra, which appears at this time each day. The people of Broome claim that certain other folk can see the vision too & that it brings them ill fortune. For this reason it is usual for Broome folk to remain within their city walls during the sunset hour.

In Broome

❦ There are no inns in Broome, as such. The many taverns are for eating & drinking only. There are, however, a number of small, furnished houses & cabins in which visitors to the town can stay, free of charge, for up to a month. The only condition is that you clean your borrowed dwelling thoroughly before you leave. My usual cabin—where I am writing these words now—is built on a mound so that it rises above the town walls & thus has a good view of the sea.

❦ Broome itself is not an old town in Deltoran terms & has few of the nooks & crannies beloved of tourists. It is sturdy, tidy & clean, but its chief attractions are its glorious setting & the character of its people. By day, explore the outdoors. By night, enjoy the company in the taverns and dance hall.

❦ The harbor fishing wharves, where the day's catch is sold, boats are cleaned, nets are mended & gossip is exchanged, are always worth a visit. Masses of seabirds throng the area, diving for scraps. Stalls sell mugs of fish soup, boiled crab claws, fish cakes & fingers of potato fried in oil, very good with a little salt.

✦ The waves of the Sea of Serpents break fiercely around Broome, but it is still possible to bathe in the shallows, if you care to brave the cold. The salt water is bracing & helps small wounds to heal.

✦ Walking along the shore is always a pleasure. This very morning, on my way to Dragon's Nest just after dawn, I saw my first Ruby dragon of this trip. She swooped down to hover over the sea not far from a lone fishing boat. I fear the fisherfolk were not as pleased to see her as I was—I could see them showing signs of anger & alarm. Then a huge sea serpent surged from the depths & loomed over their boat, snapping its fangs.

The dragon swooped, plucked the serpent from the water & flew off with it, saving the boat & a dozen lives. When I met this same dragon afterward & congratulated her, she thanked me but admitted that she had hardly noticed the boat. She was merely intent on gaining a tasty, filling meal.

Dragon's Nest

This place provides the most dramatic sight Broome has to offer. It is reached by moving north along the shoreline until sand gives way to stones & rocks. Continue over the rocks until the Barrier Mountains loom directly in front of you. Now you have reached Deltora's most easterly point & here lies Dragon's Nest, a large, deep, bowl-shaped hollow between the Barrier Mountains & the wild sea.

The hollow does indeed look like the nest of a giant dragon, being formed of round stones that have been polished smooth by water. It even has a lining of seaweed that looks from a distance very like human hair. It is a favorite dragon haunt, though I found only 1 there today—the same one who saved the fishing boat.

Set out after breakfast, carrying food & water with you & you can make a pleasant, leisurely day of it, with plenty of time to be back in Broome before the sun is too low in the sky.

The Ruby dragon snares a meal

Note: It is tempting to climb into the hollow, but only do this when the tide is falling & do not stay at the bottom too long. At high tide, great waves break over Dragon's Nest, filling it with frothing water. This is an impressive sight if seen from above, but is fearful for anyone trapped below, as I nearly was on my first visit.

Farewell to Broome

I have always said that a week's stay in Broome will revive the weariest traveler & so I have found this time. The few scratches & cuts I sustained in End Wood are healed, my feet no longer ache & the fresh sea air & good company have soothed my troubled spirit.

At dawn I will leave Broome, trek over the hills & take the Mountain Road to the north. My plan is to follow the road through the far north until it is time to turn south again to visit the city of D'Or. It is my fervent hope that by this means I will come across more Ruby dragons.

The Ruby North

I have spent my nights under the stars since leaving Broome, for the weather has been fine. I have had much on my mind & I fear I have broken my resolution to keep my notes up-to-date. Tonight I am determined to make up for lost time.

At noon today, having almost reached the Lapis Lazuli border, I turned off the Mountain Road & began moving down the Golden Way, which is the road to D'Or. I am presently camped by a stream just outside the village of Purley. The night is clear. There is a full moon & I have a lantern for extra light. The lantern is fueled by Broome fish oil, so smells rather strong, but I am grateful for it.

Here, then, are my notes on the Ruby North:

The Mountain Road is rough & rutted with cart tracks & along its length the Barrier Mountains loom darkly in the near distance. The land of the north is lush & fertile, however & traveling through it should be joyous. Many small villages—some just nameless hamlets of 3 or 4 cottages—are strung along the road like beads, most a mere day's slow ride apart.

I would be in paradise except for the worrying fact that I have seen no more dragons, though Ak-Baba I have seen in plenty.

The palace seems far away—more distant even than it seemed in Broome. Fine clothes, polite manners & formal ceremonies are unknown here. The people live simply & make their own rules.

They generally have to make their own entertainment as well, so welcome any traveler, peddler or wandering minstrel who can supply them with news and bring variety into their lives. Word of the approach of the caravans of The Masked Ones,* for example, is reason to plan a festival.

*The Masked Ones

The Masked Ones are traveling entertainers. Their troupe performs throughout the wild north of Deltora. I first saw it in Ruby territory, but I have seen it in the territories of the Opal, Lapis Lazuli & Emerald as well.

The Masked Ones are not the only performers to travel the north. I mention them in particular because:

1. They are extremely skilled—the acrobats, singers, strong men, fortune-tellers, magicians, clowns & jugglers are the best I have ever seen. Their performance is not to be missed.

2. They are highly unusual, because they wear masks—animal & bird heads so lifelike that you would think they were real. It is rumored that they never take their masks off—even in private.

3. They are a close-knit group—more like a family than an ordinary circus troupe. They do not welcome outsiders into their confidence, they do not marry outside the troupe & their lives are governed by many secret rules. They are governed by a leader who is said to have the power of life & death over them all. When not open to the public, their campsite is protected by large poison-spitting moths, the like of which I have never seen anywhere else in Deltora.

4. It is whispered that the troupe was founded by Ballum, the disgraced younger brother of King Elstred, our present king's great-grandfather. Ballum, who took to wearing a mask after his face was scarred in an accident, was once his brother's greatest friend. He was forced to flee Del & hide himself in the wilds of the north after being accused by Elstred's Chief Advisor of trying to kill Elstred out of jealousy. I am told that Ballum insisted on his innocence until his dying day.

Note: By all means go to The Masked Ones' performances if you get the chance, but do not inquire too closely into The Masked Ones' affairs, or try to find out too much about them. People they ee as spies have a way of "disappearing."

The Masked Ones

The City of D'Or

This day I reached D'Or. At this moment I am sitting on the terrace of my room in the Light-on-Water Inn—which is far too grand, in truth, to be called an inn, being more like a palace! I have bathed in warm, scented water & fed on fragrant soup, bread as light as air & fruits fresh from the D'Or orchards. After many days on the road, these comforts were very welcome.

As I look out over this city of shining towers, fountains & green spaces alive with birds, I feel that it must be as beautiful as ancient Capra was said to have been. I am no lover of great towns, but even I find it difficult not to admire the grace & loveliness of D'Or. The Ralads built it, of course—using their great talents to turn the dreams of the handsome, golden-skinned people of D'Or into a reality of brick, glass & stone.

The D'Or people came to Deltora in the time of Queen Adina, the great Adin's granddaughter. They came from across the Sea of Serpents, fleeing a terror of which they never speak. Now they are loyal citizens of Deltora & welcome travelers with open arms. All the inns & taverns are of high standard & around the same price. The people are proud & strong, but tolerant. The shopkeepers are careful & thrifty, but would regard it as dishonorable to cheat you.

Special Places of Interest

D'Or is almost like a single, beautiful sculpture. Every part of it fits so perfectly with every other part that it is difficult to advise on "special places of interest." Everywhere there are shops & studios selling the exquisite jewelry & glass for which D'Or craftsmen are well known. Everywhere there are public gardens to be enjoyed.

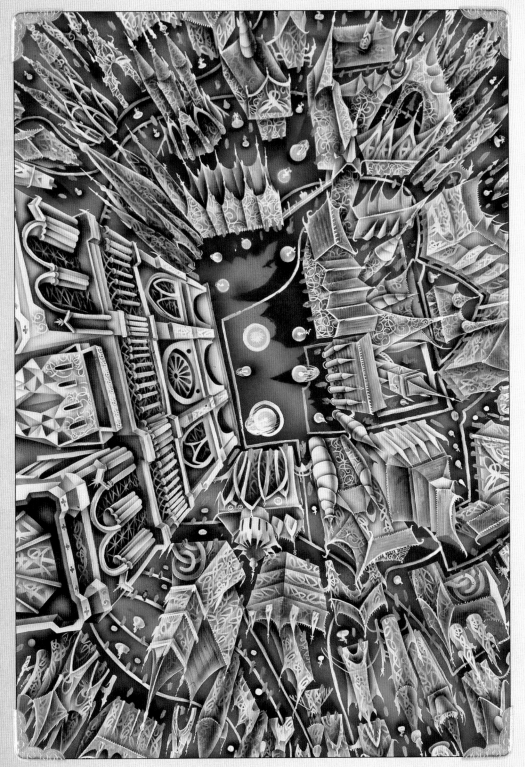

The city of D'Or, as seen from a terrace of the Light-on-Water Inn

The best thing to do, I think, is to simply wander & admire—unless you want to buy 1 of the famed D'Or horses,* in which case you must visit the great stables beside the horse fields on the city's western side.

I did exactly this earlier today, having decided to spend some of the king's gold on the means to finish my tour of Deltora more quickly than I could on foot. My horse is Pearl, a tall mare of the palest gray with white mane & tail. Pearl is strong & fast, but intelligent & steady too. She will be a good companion in the time ahead.

I will be staying in D'Or only 1 night, but many people find the city so entrancing & so full of interest that they stay at least a week—often much longer.

Note: There is little to warn you about in this city. The only important thing you can do wrong in D'Or is to willfully injure a building, plant, animal or person, or to attempt to steal a horse. People do expect visitors to be polite & to pay their bills without argument, but rudeness will not be punished—merely ignored. You should be aware, however, that if you offend in this way you will not be welcome in D'Or again.

*The Horses of D'Or

D'Or horses are fine, intelligent, spirited beasts & sell for very high prices. But be aware that not everyone is permitted to buy one. The breeders will ask any prospective buyer to ride the horse of his or her choice in a testing field. If the horse seems unhappy with its rider, or the rider does not show enough skill or understanding, no sale will be made, no matter how much gold is offered.

Some people find this difficult to accept, but there is no use arguing once a sale has been refused. The most you can hope for is that the stable master will allow you to choose another horse & try again.

Roads from D'Or

❧ The Opal Highway leads from the western side of D'Or, beyond the horse fields, into Opal territory. This is the main road out of the city & the way you should take to further explore Deltora, unless you wish to retrace your steps up the Golden Way to rejoin the Mountain Road.

❧ If you wish to return to Del across the Os-Mine Hills, turn south on the Golden Way, instead of north.

❧ Roads to the eastern farming areas exist, but they are narrow & often not in good repair. Sweetplum bushes & Traveler's Weed grow well beside these roads, but take care not to wander too far through unfamiliar ground. There is a danger of falling foul of patches of quicksand, which can be well disguised by Fool's Lawn, a type of waterweed that mimics grass. Most of these dangerous areas have warning notices, but this cannot be relied upon.*

*What to Do if You Fall into Quicksand

1. Shout for help & keep shouting. If you are traveling alone, someone may hear you & come to the rescue. A companion can pull you to safety immediately with a rope, a long stick, or even a cloak or jacket.

2. While you are waiting for help, do not struggle. The more you move, the more quickly you will sink. Try to flatten yourself on the surface, as if you are swimming.

3. Catch hold of anything that might support you, even for a few minutes, while help arrives. If you are lucky, an overhanging branch, a tree root or a clump of reeds may be within reach.

4. If you are carrying a pack, shrug it off to lighten yourself. Better to lose your belongings than your life.

Raladin

Before moving into Opal territory, I have made a short detour to the town of Raladin. This is not recommended to the general traveler. I merely note it so that these notes are a true record of my journey.

Tonight I write by candlelight in a small guest room in the home of some friends here. It is very late & the town is dark & still, but my mind is too full for sleep.

Raladin, the town of the Ralad tribe, the traditional guardians of the territory of the Ruby, is not far from D'Or. It is not signposted, is surrounded by untamed woodland & is almost impossible to find, because the Ralad people value their privacy & guard it well.

I have visited Raladin many times (by invitation) & I can tell you that it is merely a peaceful, well-ordered place of rounded earth-brick houses & halls set around a paved square with a central pool of water. Beyond the houses there are well-tended vegetable gardens & orchards. There is nothing grand to be seen & nothing exciting to be done in the evenings except to talk, play music & sing.

If this description does not content you & you still long to see Raladin with your own eyes, I urge you to restrain your impatience & wait to be invited. People who insist on trying to seek out the town sometimes meet with accidents, such as twisting their ankles on trailing vines or falling into holes.

Ralads are far from unfriendly, however & you will often meet them in your travels through their territory. You will find groups of them in other territories, too, for they are famous architects & builders & travel in teams to construct important buildings throughout Deltora. They are very easily recognized because their skins are blue-gray, their bodies are small (usually they reach only to the average man's shoulder) & they have a crest or fluff of orange-red hair on the crowns of their heads.

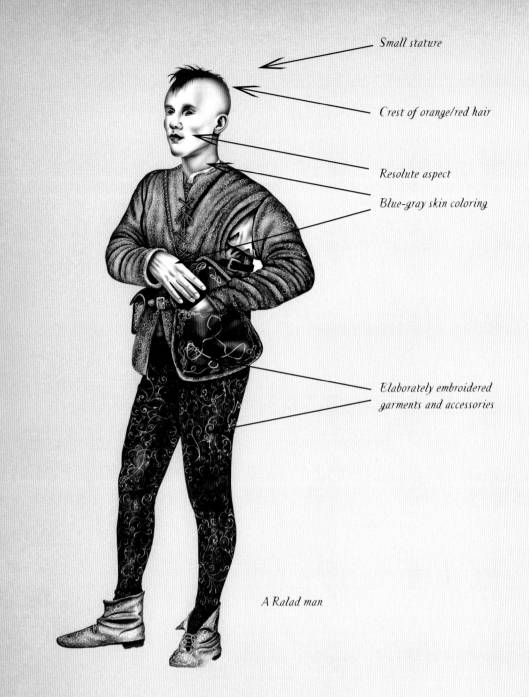

Small stature

Crest of orange/red hair

Resolute aspect

Blue-gray skin coloring

Elaborately embroidered
garments and accessories

A Ralad man

The Ralads' appearance can lead strangers to think
they are physically weak & sometimes even mentally
feeble as well! Nothing could be further from the truth.
Ralads are immensely strong for their size, extremely
skillful with their hands & very quick-witted. They
are gentle, usually happy folk who live in harmony
with nature & dislike fighting, but they are extremely
courageous & determined.

Ralad Picture Writing

The Ralad people traditionally write in pictures or symbols. There are many thousands of Ralad symbols. Here are a few common ones with their meanings:

1. day/life	*2. family*	*3. one/one person/only*	*4. I/me/my*
5. you/your	*6. the great Adin*	*7. bird/freedom*	*8. travel/go to*
9. child/heir	*10. save from death*	*11. friend/friends*	*12. plus/with/as well as*
13. fast/urgent	*14. home*	*15. the Belt of Deltora*	*16. sleep*
17. music	*18. equals/leads to/causes*	*19. food*	*20. drink*
21. stop/forbid/banish	*22. happy*	*23. sad*	*24. Ak-Baba*

Adult Ralads combine symbols for greater speed & clarity—the symbol for "my" is drawn inside the symbol for "life" to make the phrase "my life," for example.

Young Ralad children & others (like myself) who are still learning Ralad writing just use the basic symbols to make their sentences. The results read clumsily, but the meaning can usually be understood.

I arrived in Raladin in time to share the evening meal in the house of my friends & once happy greetings had been exchanged (for I have not visited the town for over 2 years) we began at once to talk of the dwindling Ruby dragon population.

We talked long into the night. The Ralads are as worried & distressed about the problem as I am. Unlike most other Deltorans they neither fear nor hate dragons. They believe, as I do, that the fates of the land & the dragons are linked.

They were not surprised to hear that I had seen only 1 Ruby dragon so far on my journey. They believe that only 2 survive in the whole of the territory! Reports from their building teams in other territories say that the case is just as bad elsewhere. They have written to King Lucan & received a reply thanking them for their message & saying that their request would be attended to when time allows.

In the morning I return to D'Or & from there set out for the territory of the Opal. For once I will be leaving Raladin with a heavy heart.

8.

Opal Territory

> People flying!
> Hira burning!
> The wings of flame
> Cry despairing the blaze!
>
> Opal dragon prophecy

Opal Dragons

Color: scales gleam with every color of the rainbow.
Characteristics: serious, formal, cautious, far-seeing. Prefer planning to impulsive action. The best eyesight of all the dragon tribes.
Recent sighting: the Hira Plain.
Food: Muddlet foals, Pinwheel Vipers, rats, River Broad fish (but not Wise Fish*). Fighting Spiders are considered a sweetmeat & are usually taken in pairs.

A day's brisk walk along the Opal Highway from D'Or will bring you to the shallow stream that marks the end of Ruby territory. If you are on horseback, as I am, or traveling in a carriage or cart, you will of course reach the border more quickly.

When you have crossed the stream, you are in Opal territory. This is the home of the Plains tribe & is therefore commonly known in Deltora as the territory of the Plains. There are many villages & farms in the land of the Opal, but there is only 1 main center—the city of Hira, which stands alone on a fertile plain in a bend of the mighty River Broad.

Follow the Opal Highway for a little longer & you will reach a place where it splits into 2 narrower roads. One road leads due south to the market town of Miller's Rise, the other to the River & the city of Hira.

Which Way to Go?

Here are your choices:

1. If you wish to return to Del, or to cut short your time
in Opal territory, turn left down the Miller's Rise track.
After you have passed through the hilly country in which
Miller's Rise is nestled, you will enjoy an easy walk
through peaceful farmland to Deltora Way. A turn left at
Deltora Way will lead you directly back to Del. A right
turn will take you into the west.

   Note: As noted previously, travelers on Deltora Way
are sometimes troubled by bandits. Follow the advice
given in Bandits, Thieves & Pirates, on pages 18 & 19.

2. If you are interested in cities & wish to go directly
to Hira, take the right-hand track to the River Broad.
When you have reached the Broad you will see Hira in the
distance on the other side. Ring the bell that hangs from
a post on the riverbank & sooner or later a boat or barge
will come to ferry you across the water.

   A few silver coins will usually be enough to pay for the
trip across, though I am told that a gold coin is now being
demanded for the return journey. This is scandalous, but
Hira's leaders have more important things to worry about
than the dishonesty of a few boatmen, it seems.

   Naturally you will have to leave horses, carts &
carriages behind. Do not fear theft—this part of the
riverbank is quite safe & there is grass on which horses
can graze until your return.

3. If you wish to see some of the most beautiful wild
places in Opal territory (which is naturally what I would
advise & what I myself am doing), go to the River Broad
& instead of crossing it follow it north till it meets the

Mountain Road. You can then cross the river by its only bridge, constructed (of course) by the builders of Raladin.

After this you can either continue straight along the Mountain Road into Lapis Lazuli country, stopping on the way at pleasant small towns like Happy Vale & Charity, or you can move south again to the Hira plain.

Note: I advise against staying in any of the inns you may come across as you move up the river. The riverbank inns are all very small & do not welcome strangers. If any of them agree to take you for the night, it is 10 to 1 that you will be robbed before morning. You will also find that the beds are lumpy & crawling with bugs & the food you are served is of the worst quality.

It is far better to make camp beside the stream & enjoy a good meal from the supplies you have brought with you from D'Or. This is what I have done. It is good to be sitting beneath the stars once more, after some nights spent confined within 4 walls.

I will sleep now. At dawn I will travel on up the river in the hope that I will find an Opal dragon fishing for breakfast.

The River Broad— General Information

❧ The River Broad is very wide & deep. It rises in the Barrier Mountains & after bending around Hira flows on through the land of the Lapis Lazuli & into the territory of the Amethyst. There it joins the River Tor on its way to the Silver Sea.

❧ Broad water is perfectly fit to drink in Opal territory. You will find it very cold & pure.

❧ Take great care when bathing in the Broad. Stay close to the bank & keep a hand on a secure rock or tree at all times. The water flows extremely quickly & it is easy to be swept away.

❧ Fishing is good, but there are certain very large silver fish (known as Wise Fish*) that you should not attempt to catch under any circumstances.

*Wise Fish

The River Broad fish known as Wise Fish are extremely large. Most I have seen are longer than my arm & the largest are as fat as a Muddlet foal. They do not appear to live anywhere else but in that part of the Broad that flows through Opal territory.

Wise Fish

Wise Fish are far too cunning to take a baited hook & will break through any net, but you should not attempt to catch them by any means. The local folk consider it very bad luck to injure a Wise Fish. There are many old tales of foolish hunters who speared Wise Fish close to the bank. It is said that most of these hunters were dragged to their deaths in the river when the speared fish dived. Those few who survived all drowned, apparently by accident, not long afterward.

Local legend has it that Wise Fish have long memories, never forget an injury to a member of their tribe & will sooner or later take revenge on anyone who tries to do them harm. It is also said that Wise Fish, if treated with respect, will actually help a human in trouble. Along the river tales abound of small children rescued from drowning & boats saved from sinking by clusters of Wise Fish working together.

I have never witnessed any such events during my visits to Opal territory, but strange as they sound, I am certain that the stories are true. Opal dragons do not hunt Wise Fish, but hold them in great esteem, regarding them as guardians of the river.

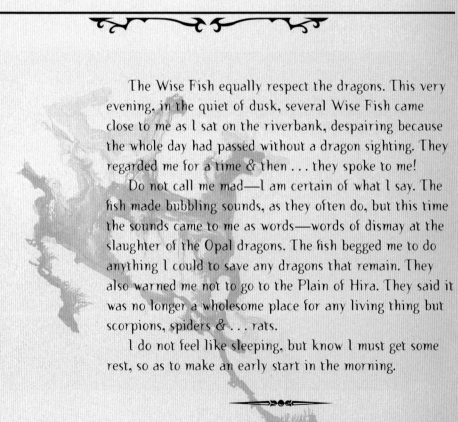

The Wise Fish equally respect the dragons. This very evening, in the quiet of dusk, several Wise Fish came close to me as I sat on the riverbank, despairing because the whole day had passed without a dragon sighting. They regarded me for a time & then . . . they spoke to me!

Do not call me mad—I am certain of what I say. The fish made bubbling sounds, as they often do, but this time the sounds came to me as words—words of dismay at the slaughter of the Opal dragons. The fish begged me to do anything I could to save any dragons that remain. They also warned me not to go to the Plain of Hira. They said it was no longer a wholesome place for any living thing but scorpions, spiders & . . . rats.

I do not feel like sleeping, but know I must get some rest, so as to make an early start in the morning.

Dangers of Opal Territory

I have just ridden another whole day along the riverbank road without sighting a single dragon. The farmers & laborers I met along the way agreed that dragon numbers have dropped dramatically in the past few months. This pleased them immensely. It also pleased them to tell me that there are rumors of bad trouble in Hira. Folk on this side of the river have no time for city dwellers.

Various adventures during today's trek have reminded me that I should warn you of certain dangers you will encounter in Opal territory. I should have mentioned them at the beginning, but my mind was too full of the problem of the dragons.

❦ **Plains Scorpions** may be found everywhere in this territory. They are easily identified, being purple with black stripes & as large as a man's fist. They are extremely aggressive & their stings are always fatal. They like to hide in dim places. Inspect sleeping blankets carefully before using them. Stamp on the toes of boots & shake the boots out, before putting them on. Do not leave garments on the ground—hang them from a tree or pack them away.

I forgot this last rule myself today & it nearly cost me my life. I

Plains Scorpion

carelessly threw my coat down when I stopped to brew tea at midday. When I reached for the coat again a little later I narrowly avoided being bitten by a scorpion that had crawled into the sleeve. I crushed the scorpion with this book, which I happened to have in my hand at the time. (I had been reading my notes of yesterday while drinking my tea.) Hence the unpleasant stain on the previous page, for which I apologize.

❦ **Pinwheel Vipers** are as thin as a finger but about as long as a man's arm & extremely venomous. They are most often found lying in the sun in the neat, flat coil that gives them their name. They are hard to see because they

Pinwheel Vipers

change color according to their background—on grass they are green, on bare earth they are brown, etc. Today I saw a viper that had turned bright blue to match its bed of Brighteyes. (Brighteyes is a creeping, small-leaved plant that grows well along the River Broad & is in flower now. The leaves, when dried, crushed & soaked in cold tea, make a comforting dressing for blisters.)

Pinwheel Vipers will strike instantly if trodden on, aiming for the ankles or shins. This is why high boots or leggings are particularly useful in this territory.

If someone in your party is bitten, wash the wound & bind it tightly. Give a double portion of snakebite remedy (which you should be carrying, if you have followed my instructions on essential equipment) & keep the patient as still as possible for at least 24 hours. If the patient survives this period, he or she will live, though weakness & numbness of the bitten limb may persist for months afterward.

❧ **Scarlet Night** is a red fungus that covers the inside walls of some caves in the purple hills on the east side of River Broad. When fresh, Scarlet Night is deadly to the touch. A single smear on bare skin will kill. There is no cure. Smeared clothing may be removed without risk after 10 minutes. The fungus loses its potency very quickly.

❧ **Muddlets*** are not dangerous individually, but a Muddlet stampede is fearful. If you see a large Muddlet herd, keep alert. The beasts are unpredictable & easily startled. The only reliable escape from a stampede is to climb a tree, to flatten yourself at the bottom of a deep ditch or, if you are near enough, to run for the river.

❧ **Fighting Spiders** are heavily built & as large as the average woman's spread hand. They may be brown, gray or black & often bear spots, stripes or other markings in lighter colors. They are not venomous but can still deliver a powerful, painful bite that can quickly become infected. They will attack any creature, but are most aggressive to their own kind. Two Fighting Spiders will fight each other to the death, unless prevented. They may be found in the territories of the Lapis Lazuli & the Diamond, but are most numerous in the land of the Opal, particularly on the Hira Plain.

Fighting Spider numbers have been gradually dwindling, because too many are being caught & sold. Captured spiders are bought by dolts who keep them as pets. Owners allow their spiders to fight each other, betting on the outcome of the battle. A champion Fighting Spider can earn much gold for its owner, who must handle it with thick leather gloves to avoid being bitten.

Fighting Spiders out on the Hira Plain

✦ **Bees** can also be very aggressive in Opal territory, particularly on the northern edge of the Hira Plain. They usually keep to themselves, but will come at you in a swarm if angered. Do not attempt to rob beehives in Opal territory. Honey can be purchased easily enough.

✦ **Plains Rats** are extremely large & aggressive. Keep your pack tightly sealed or they will steal your supplies. They were becoming a particular problem in Hira the last time I visited & I gather they are now out of control.

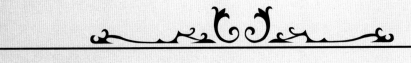

Muddlets

Muddlets are only found in Opal territory & I believe are unusual enough to deserve a special note. They are as large as horses, but have only 3 legs—one at the front & 2 at the back, so that they move with an odd, rocking gait. They have long, floppy ears & their hides are splashed & striped in many different colors.

Muddlets: strong, fast and colorful, but very unreliable

Muddlets roam wild in large herds all over Opal territory. Some, whose ancestors were caught & tamed long ago, are used by Plains farmers for riding & for drawing carts & ploughs.

The farmers claim that Muddlets are more useful than horses. Certainly they are very strong & speedy, but they lack the intelligence of horses & are so extremely willful that they can be quite unreliable & even dangerous, in my opinion. They will bolt, for example, if they smell overripe apples, which are their favorite food. They will also bolt when nearing their home field, or if startled.

If you are traveling Opal territory on foot, you will almost certainly be offered a Muddlet sometime during your visit. The price may seem to you very low, but I advise you not to be tempted. I made the mistake once & will never do it again.

The Muddlet I bought was impossible to control & bolted over a low cliff in an attempt to reach an orchard on the other side of a gap. The fall nearly killed us both. No sooner had the Muddlet recovered than it lolloped away—either to try for the apples again, or to go back to its previous owner. By that time I did not care where it went. I was glad to see the back of it.

A Note in Haste...

On waking this morning I caught a distant glimpse of an Opal dragon in the skies above the plain on the other side of the river. I have decided to cross the river at once, abandoning my plan to ride all the way to the bridge.

A farmer is lending me a boat & will care for Pearl until my return. I am thankful that for once I have the gold to pay for services like these. I will be leaving as soon as the boat is ready . . .

The Hira Plain

The news is bad—very bad. I managed to reach the other
side of the river while the dragon was still hunting &
was able to attract his attention, thanks to his excellent
eyesight. He told me that he is the last of the Opal
dragons. His father, the tribe's most ancient member & my
dear friend, died of natural causes 3 months ago, sadly
weakened by grief. The rest have been killed by Ak-Baba.

The dragon (whose secret name of course I cannot tell
you) could tell me little of the fates of the neighboring
dragon tribes—except the dreadful news that he saw a
Ruby dragon killed only 2 days ago, while he was near the
Ruby border.

He told me this quite calmly. Clearly it never occurred
to him to go to his Ruby cousin's aid. Like many humans,
he cares only for the fortunes of his own tribe.

I told him that the fortunes of all were linked. I told
him I was sure that the destruction of Deltora's dragons
was a Shadowlands plot to strip the land of its most fierce
protectors.

He thought carefully, as Opal dragons do & at last said
he already felt a wicked presence in his land. The evil was
hidden in the city of Hira, he said. It had begun small,
weak & young—so weak & young that at first the Opal
dragons paid no heed to it. They believed the people of
Hira would deal with it.

The dragons would not attack the city—not for
something so apparently unimportant. Since the time of
Adin, no Opal dragon has harmed a human in its territory.

But the hidden menace was growing, he said & the
people of Hira were doing nothing to stop it. Indeed, they
seemed unaware of it. For years they had been concerned
only with trying to control the rat plague.

"But they have failed," the dragon told me. "The city

is overrun. It will be abandoned, very soon. Then I will tear down its walls & destroy the evil within it. This I have sworn."

I did not say aloud the thought that instantly came to me, but the dragon seemed to know it without a word being spoken. "'If I survive for long enough," he added. "But I am hopeful that I will. I am taking great care."

He left me then, to go back to his hunting. Filled with terrible despair I stood alone on the plain—the historic plain where a great battle was fought, the Belt of Deltora was at last made complete & the Shadow Lord's hordes were vanquished.

The plain is peaceful. The grass reaches to my knees & ripples in the wind. Muddlets are drinking at the river, or grazing on the leaves pulled from the lowest branches of the trees. But there are far fewer Muddlets than when last I came here.

In the distance the city hulks dark, cold & silent. I would think it was deserted if it were not for the smoke rising from a few chimneys. No flags fly from its battlements. The fields of wheat, corn & oats that checkered the ground around it on my last visit look dull & brown instead of green & gold.

What has happened here? How could a few rats cause such a change in a great city?

Much as I dislike the place, I must go & see for myself.

The City of Hira

It is some days since I have picked up my pen, but I can no longer delay making my report on Hira.

I write this by lantern light. I am camped by the River Broad Bridge, having crossed the river once more, reclaimed Pearl & hastened north. In the morning I will join the Mountain Road & travel west to Lapis Lazuli territory. I will go as fast as Pearl can carry me. I am

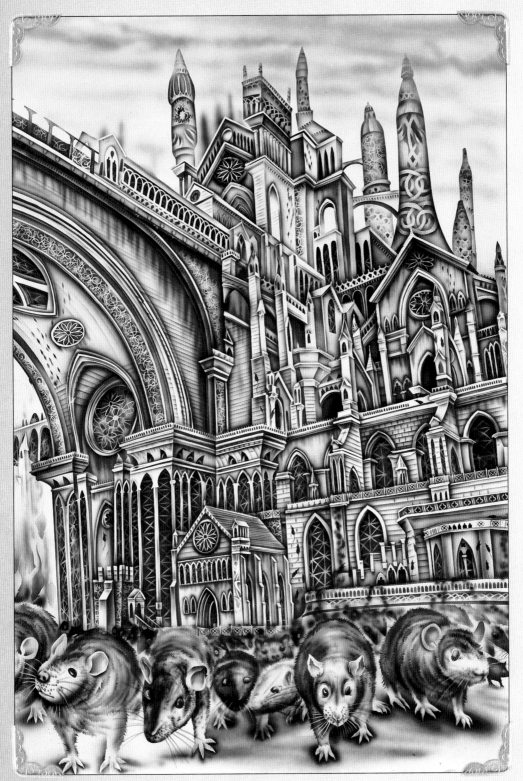

Hira: The City of the Rats

shaken by what I have seen & heard in the land of the
Opal & wish to stay in it no longer than I have to.

I spent but a single hour in the wretched city on the
plain & that hour was too long. I would not have believed
the change in the place if I had not seen it with my own
eyes.

It is years since I visited Hira. It has always been too
closed in, too dim & airless, for my liking, being mostly
roofed & more like one huge, maze-like building than a
city. It is always lit by torches, even by day. Still, it was
Adin's base during the final battle against the Shadow
Lord, so it is of great historical interest. In addition,
many folk find its carved stonework, high arches, massive
fireplaces & vast Great Hall impressive.

Another attraction has always been the food—the
Hira cooks are justly famous for the delicacies they
produce. Hira is also well known for its many gem traders
& jewelers.

Once, then, it might have been worth a visit. This is
no longer the case.

The city is swarming with huge red-eyed rats. The
shadows writhe with them, the place stinks of them. The
sound of the creatures scuttling endlessly in the walls is
enough to drive anyone mad.

All business, trade & farming has stopped. The people,
thin & gaunt, are consumed by their battle against the
rats, which eat their food, destroy their possessions, attack
their children & spread disease.

They are in despair. I cannot count the number of
times I heard people cry: "King Brandon could have
helped. But he did not seem to understand how bad the
situation was. Neither did King Lucan, who is now too
weak & ill to help in any case."

The city leaders, always so cold & dignified, so
superior to all others, are now desperate & it seems to me,
half mad. Three-quarters of them have died of rat-borne
diseases & have not been replaced. The few who remain
alive still wear the stiff golden wigs that are their badges
of offices, but their richly embroidered robes no longer

Hira city leaders

sweep the ground for fear of the rats that seethe on the floors.

Their power is gone, in any case. The people they once ruled have lost faith in them. All authority in the city has passed to the rat catchers, whose word is law.

It will not be long, I think, before the Opal dragon's prophecy is fulfilled & Hira is abandoned. The people's spirits are broken. In their despair, they have come to believe that the city is cursed—that the rat plague is punishment for their wickedness . . . though when I asked what that wickedness was, they did not know.

Stay away from Hira. Once it was great, but its greatness has ended. Its people will soon be gone. It has become the City of the Rats.

9.

Lapis Lazuli Territory

Scaly superstition blazes!
Mere dragons each
Burn of word prey,
Burn first dragonsong.

Traditional Lapis Lazuli dragon hunting song

Lapis Lazuli Dragons

Color: midnight blue with silver "stars."
Characteristics: quick-witted, impulsive, curious, amusing, easily bored. Enjoy songs & risk-taking. Smaller & daintier than members of other dragon tribes, but faster in flight.
Recent sighting: the Shifting Sands.
Food: cold-blooded creatures, notably Sand Beasts (which have increased vastly in number since Lapis Lazuli dragons have become fewer), fish, lizards & snakes.

I crossed the border into Lapis Lazuli territory as the sun was setting. I have now made camp for the night. The Mountains loom to the north, dark against the gray sky.

I stopped briefly at the Opal town of Happy Vale on my way here, so am well supplied with bread, cheese, apples, honey & fresh water.

The folk in Happy Vale had heard that the rat plague in Hira had grown worse, but like the riverbank farmers they did not seem troubled. Most of them have never been to the city in their lives. The few that have visited it have brought back tales of dimness, bustle, endless rules, stale air, overrich food & gold-wigged leaders who think themselves very important & sneer at country folk.

Before dawn tomorrow I will go directly to the only place in this territory where I am certain to find surviving Lapis Lazuli dragons—the forbidden desert known as the Shifting Sands. A signposted track to the Sands branches off the Mountain Road.

My task tonight is to make some general notes
on Lapis Lazuli territory. I must not forget that this
journey's purpose is to write a guide for travelers. I have
already spent a great deal of the king's gold & I have a
duty to complete the task I was appointed to do.

Lapis Lazuli Territory—
General Notes

❧ Lapis Lazuli territory is generally rich & fertile. It is
the ancient home of the Mere tribe, though these days it
is also home to many folk who originally came from other
parts of Deltora, or from across the sea.

❧ It is a land of scattered villages, farms, horses &
small silver-mining towns. It has only 1 main center—
the large, colorful town of Rithmere, which lies
beside the River Broad not far from the Opal
border.

❧ Mere folk are hot-blooded & superstitious. The love
of gambling seems to be in their blood. Most will bet on
anything at all, though cards, dice, wrestling matches
& horse races are favorites. They have a long tradition
of being fierce fighters, but since the time of Adin they
accept most visiting strangers with good humor. They are,
however, still suspicious of Plains people, their eastern
neighbors & ancient enemies.

❧ There are many good camping spots throughout the
territory—some in spectacular places. For example, if you
choose to remain on the Mountain Road instead of visiting
Rithmere, you will come across a spot known as The
Funnel not far from the Emerald border. Here a waterfall
thunders down into a vast rock basin. Foaming water spins
in the basin like a whirlpool before draining away. It is a
breathtaking sight.

❧ Inns & taverns are of variable quality & some are nothing but dingy gambling dens. A quick way of judging a Lapis Lazuli inn is the condition of the long white apron always worn by the landlord or landlady as a badge of office. If the apron is gray & covered with old stains, move on. If the apron is basically clean, the inn is worth trying.

Mere Superstitions

There are hundreds of these, but here are some you must know:

❧ When you partly spill your drink, ill fortune will result unless you immediately drink all that remains in your cup & turn your cup upside down.

❧ You must never state your plans for the morrow as if they were certain. You should always say, "*All being well*, I am going to do this or that tomorrow."

❧ Become accustomed to the fact that the skins of Lapis Adders are extremely powerful (& costly) talismans. Skins are passed down through the generations in Mere families & worn with pride, usually dangling from the belt. Never show disgust when you notice this.

❧ King rats should not be killed by any means other than drowning or your home will become rat-infested.

❧ The worst thing you can do in a Mere home is to sneeze 3 times in a row. If this happens you should go outside at once, turn around 3 times, then come back in by the same door. If you neglect to do this, you will bring bad luck to everyone in the house.

❧ Belt, ears, neck, hair & clothing are always hung with lucky charms* as protection against a multitude of ills & to bring good fortune. Small engraved silver or clay

charms are sold everywhere in Lapis Lazuli territory.
You should buy a few & display them or Mere folk will
shun you as unlucky.

Some people of the Mere

✢ Will you be offended if a stranger taps you on the nose in
the street? No, because it simply means that the stranger's
shadow has fallen across your own, which is bad luck. If he
or she quickly taps your nose bad luck is avoided.

✢ Be aware that it is considered very unlucky to step on
a mouse. (Tell no one if this happens to you by accident.)

✢ Put sand in your boots at night to ensure sound sleep.

✢ Around Mere houses & public buildings plants never
grow because the earth is regularly scattered with salt to
ward off bad luck.

✢ Your best defense against illness is to carry a clove of
garlic in your pocket.

✢ Waist-length hair is considered to bring good fortune
to both males & females.

*Mere Lucky Charms

During their lifetimes, Mere folk buy as many charms as they can afford. Some people have hundreds & jingle as they walk. The silver charms are of course far more expensive than the clay ones & thought to be far more powerful. The charms are usually threaded on thin strips of leather.

Here are some of the most common:

cup—will ensure you never go thirsty	bread—will ensure you never go hungry	snake with tail in its mouth— will protect from snakebite
heart—will ensure love comes to you & remains	coin—will bring money	dagger—offers protection against violent attack
fireplace—ensures peace & comfort in the home	cradle—brings & protects children	die—brings luck in gambling

General Warnings

❈ If you loathe the sight of gambling it would be best for you to continue west along the Mountain Road into Emerald territory, leaving the land of the Lapis Lazuli behind you as quickly as possible. There is no escaping gambling here.

❈ Read my list of Mere superstitions & take good note of them. It is unwise to do anything that folk in this territory regard as bad luck.

❈ Keep your money belt well hidden & bar your door at night if staying in an inn. Sneak thieves & pickpockets abound in Lapis Lazuli territory, especially in Rithmere. It is unusual, however, for money to be taken by force.

❈ Do not be drawn into gambling games unless you have money you are happy to lose. Most of the tavern card & dice games in country areas are honest, but you will often find yourself playing with experts who make their living by winning. In Rithmere, cheating & trickery are commonplace.

❈ It is not recommended that you drink River Broad water in Lapis Lazuli territory without boiling it first.

❈ Several varieties of venomous snakes & lizards are to be found in the territory.* Keep your snakebite remedy handy.

*Dangerous Reptiles

Lapis Lazuli territory is well known for its many venomous snakes & lizards. The most common are listed below.

1. **Lapis Adders,** sometimes called "**Lucky Snakes,**" are dark blue with silver flecks that glitter in sun or moonlight. They are small, fast-moving snakes that strike with astonishing speed when angered or startled & will bite again & again until their venom sacs are exhausted. They are found throughout the territory, but particularly in the grasslands of the north.

It is considered lucky to see a Lapis Adder—though it is far from lucky to be bitten by one. Lapis Adder bites are very painful & are always accompanied by a blinding headache.

2. **Mouse Banes** are black-&-white-striped lizards that are about as big as large domestic cats. They mainly hunt mice & so can be found anywhere in town or country where mice are common, such as barns, stables, food stores & badly-kept taverns.

Mouse Banes are extremely aggressive. They have snake-like fangs as well as grinding teeth & can inject potent venom that causes high fever & painful swelling.

Mouse Bane

3. **Spitfire Dragons** are so called because they spit fiery venom & look a little like miniature dragons. Of course they are no relation to real dragons at all, but are a kind of lizard. The folds on their backs are not wings, but merely flaps of skin that puff up when the lizards are attacking prey or defending themselves. Spitfire Dragons can be as long as a 2-year-old Muddlet calf. Their scales are dull gray-blue, brightening instantly to shining silver when the creatures spit.

Spitfire Dragon

Spitfire Dragons are mostly found in the north of Lapis Lazuli territory & usually inhabit rocky places. They generally prey on birds & the young of other lizards & snakes, but will spit poison at any creature that moves close to them. The venom does not blister, but it has a numbing, paralyzing effect that soon spreads through the entire body if not washed away speedily.

4. **River Wares** are blind water snakes that are found not only in & around the River Broad in Lapis Lazuli territory, but around smaller streams as well. They are so colorless as to be almost invisible in water. They hunt by vibration & sound & will leap out of the water to strike at prey such as hovering birds or unwary humans leaning over a stream to fill a water bottle.

5. **Scorpion Lizards** are found only in the Shifting Sands. They are scarlet to match the color of the sand in which they live & have long blue tongues, which they use to snap Dune Flies from the air. They look quite harmless but are in fact quite capable of killing—not with their teeth, though these are sharp, but with a small poisonous barb at the end of the tail.

Faced with what it sees as danger, the Scorpion Lizard will catch hold of its enemy with teeth and front claws & curve its tail under its body to sting with astonishing speed. The venom can kill a hunting bird & make a human extremely ill, but has no effect on Sand Beasts, which eat Scorpion Lizards by the hundred.

Note: If a member of your party is bitten by any snake or lizard in Lapis Lazuli territory, immediately wash & bind the wound & give a dose of snakebite remedy according to the directions on the bottle. Keep the patient still for 8 hours, after which time he or she will either have died or be well enough to travel on.

It is now very late. I have written long into the night
& feel that I have done my duty for once. In the morning,
the Shifting Sands . . .

━━━━◆━━━━

The Shifting Sands

This large expanse of red sand dunes lies strangely in
the fertile northern half of Lapis Lazuli territory. It is
a perilous place. The Mere people regard it as forbidden
& leave it strictly alone. They do not like to be reminded
that in their old, savage days they used it to dispose of the
worst of their criminals & prisoners taken during border
wars with the Plains tribe.

The Shifting Sands

The Sands have been fully explored by only 1 person—a woman who lived before the time of Adin. Her name was Rigane. She was usually known as "Rigane the Mad" (it seems to be the fate of we explorers to be called mad!). Rigane's notes on her journeys into the Sands were copied into the *Deltora Annals,* so are freely available to anyone who cares to go to the palace library & read them.

You will know that you have nearly reached the Sands when you come across an ancient engraved warning stone. The Sands themselves cannot be seen from the road. Long before the time of Adin vast boulders were piled up around the dunes to wall them off from the rest of the land. The wall was raised to stop the growth of the Sands, it is said—as if the Sands were alive.

I am sitting now on top of that ancient wall of stones, watching for dragons. It is noon. Surely, if I wait long enough, a dragon will come. There are vast, insect-like, mirror-eyed monsters in the dunes—the Mere people call them Sand Beasts*—and Lapis Lazuli dragons relish Sand Beasts above every other food.

* Terreocti (Sand Beasts)

Terreocti, more commonly known as "Sand Beasts," have increased in number since I was last at the Shifting Sands. I can only imagine that this is because in these days there are fewer Lapis Lazuli dragons to eat them.

Sand Beasts are fascinating creatures. Adults are as tall as 3 men & look like monstrous insects. They have 8 jointed, spiny legs, the lowest pair of legs bearing claws, the other 3 pairs tipped by cutting pincers. The head is small & dominated by masses of mirror-like eyes. I have never been able to count the number of eyes, though I have tried many times.

Each Sand Beast carries several leathery, sack-like stomachs on the front of its body. When a stomach is full it tears away from the body & falls to the ground. The Sand Beast then lays an egg inside the stomach & leaves its young to develop alone, knowing that it will have a good food supply when it hatches.

Sand Beasts will eat anything. They hide beneath the sand & spring out to catch their prey with appalling efficiency. Scorpion Lizards (described earlier) are their chief source of food.

My sketch (no doubt redrawn by a competent artist by the time you see it) will give you some idea of what a Sand Beast looks like. Just imagining being caught in the pincers of a creature like this will surely make you realize that walking in the Shifting Sands is not an occupation for the sensible traveler.

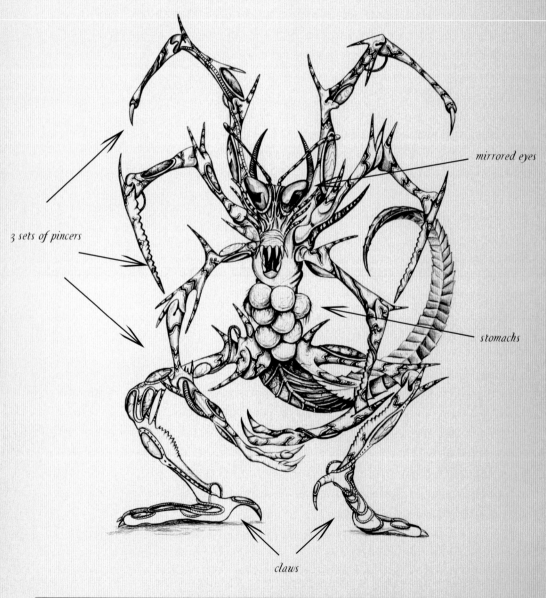

mirrored eyes

3 sets of pincers

stomachs

claws

I have been a little way into the Shifting Sands in the past, but I would not go again, and I do not recommend that you try it. The sun glares down on the parched sand, walking is very hard & you are tormented by stinging red Dune Flies. Not to mention that you are in constant danger of being ambushed by a Sand Beast.

In addition, it cannot be denied that there is a strange, unpleasant feeling to this place. A low humming sound fills the air & it seems to have a hypnotizing effect. The longer you remain in the Sands, the more you feel a compulsion to move forward. It is as if you are being drawn toward the center, which the explorer Rigane called "The Hive."

This compulsion is extremely dangerous. Not just because of Sand Beasts, but because the sand lives up to its name, quaking & shifting without warning. It is perilous to light a campfire—the sand seems to resent it. Ferocious sandstorms are common. If you survive a shifting or a storm without being smothered, you may find yourself lost, for the dunes around you will have changed shape & all footprints will have vanished.

It is far better, surely, to sit on the wall & look at the view. You will see rolling red sand, Dune Flies, Scorpion Lizards & Sand Beasts in plenty.

As I sit here now I see slight movement in a dune, above the place where a particularly large lizard is catching flies. Just a faint trickle of sand, but . . . yes!

In a great spray of sand, a Sand Beast springs from inside the dune.

It captures the lizard in its pincers.

The lizard fights for its life, doubling itself to sting.

Sand pouring from its spiny joints, the beast calmly tears its prey in half & begins to eat.

And from the sky, hurtling through the shimmering heat haze like a shooting star, plummets a midnight blue dragon, silver points flashing, talons outstretched . . .

The Road to Rithmere

It is night. I am sitting in a small attic room in an inn on the Rithmere Road. I came upon the inn (called The Traveler's Rest) as darkness fell. The lighted windows & the smells of a crackling fire & good beef stew tempted me to stop. The landlady's cheery welcome—& her spotlessly clean apron—persuaded me to stay.

The stew tasted as good as it smelled, the fire was warm & the ale was excellent. It is noisy downstairs, where folk are betting on a series of battles between 2 champion Fighting Spiders. But here in my attic, with the door firmly closed & locked, I am at peace to write.

I did not leave the Shifting Sands till the sun was low in the sky. I wished to talk to the dragon of the Lapis Lazuli but knew I should not hail her until she had finished her Sand Beast meal. This is a politeness expected by dragons, who do not enjoy talking while they eat. So I sat quietly sketching as the dragon crunched spiny limbs with relish.

Closer to me, Dune Flies were making a meal of the Sand Beast's severed head, which the dragon had tossed aside. Earlier I had seen Dune Flies being eaten by Scorpion Lizards, and a Scorpion Lizard being eaten by a Sand Beast. And now I was watching part of a Sand Beast being eaten by Dune Flies.

So the circle of life goes on.

At last the dragon was ready for conversation. She came to me, clearly very pleased to see me. We talked for a long time.

I know this dragon very well. Like all of her tribe she is a lighthearted soul who is always excellent company, but the news she had to tell me was very bad. Two days ago she found her mate lying dead on the Sands, his body covered with feasting flies & lizards.

"I went to the trouble of scaring the creatures off," she said, shrugging with pretended carelessness. "I thought I might as well, though my mate* was feeling

Sand Beast and Scorpion Lizard

nothing. Ak-Baba had torn his body, so he had left it. The Sands have claimed it now."

*Note: Actually she did not say "my mate," but used his true name aloud, which showed the depth of her emotion.

No jokes or pretended carelessness could hide the dragon's sorrow—or her fear. "In the last moon cycle I have seen only 2 other members of my tribe," she told me. "One was my mate, who now flies with our ancestors above the clouds. What if the other is dead also? What if I am the last Lapis Lazuli dragon left alive?"

I could say little to comfort her. I thought that what she feared was all too likely. I told her I would return to her as soon as I could, but that now I had to go. Not just because I have a promise to keep & a book to write, but also because I must find out if the dragon tribes in the last 3 gem territories are in the same desperate state as the tribes of the Lapis Lazuli, the Opal, the Ruby & the Topaz.

I told her to take great care. And then, reluctantly, I left her.

I am tired now & very troubled. I will sleep & hope that I do not dream. In the morning I will hasten along the road to Rithmere. I would rather go straight to Emerald territory, but this cannot be. Those who read this book will find it very strange if the great town of the Mere is not mentioned & I cannot pretend that I have visited it on this journey when I have not. Lying leaves a sour taste in my mouth.

Rithmere

Rithmere is a walled town. Its large wooden gates are guarded by soldiers wearing the traditional black leather armor & helmets of the Mere. As you pass through the gates, you will be given a silver-painted star marked with the date & time of your arrival. You will then be told to go directly to the Star House to get a permit to remain in the town.

Traveler at the Rithmere gates

The narrow streets of Rithmere are lined with shops & stalls. Peddlers, music-makers, fortune-tellers, acrobats & tricksters offering gambling games throng every corner. Hot, salty tidbits & sweet drinks are available in abundance. You will have to visit a tavern to get a drink of water or a plain, filling meal.

But before you do anything else you must visit the Star House as directed. Do not neglect to do this. If you are discovered in the streets without a permit more than half an hour after your arrival you will be heavily fined, or even imprisoned.

The Star House

The Star House is a large, square building in the town center. All roads lead to it, so you will have no trouble finding it.

A number of soldiers guard the building. They can direct you to the room where the permits are given out.

In the permit room an official will ask your name, where you have come from, the reason for your visit to Rithmere & how long you intend to stay.

There will be no difficulty in obtaining a permit unless you admit to having spent time in Opal territory (which the official will call the Plains). Then you will be taken to another, smaller room, searched & asked a great many more time-wasting questions. The Mere distrust all their neighbors, but particularly the territory to their east.

I have said that I dislike lying, but in this case I think a lie is justified. The officials expect it anyway & will help you by asking if you approached the city from the north, west or south. Murmur "north" (which is true, if you have come from the Shifting Sands) & they will be satisfied. They are busy & do not want the extra work involved in questioning a visitor from the east. They know in their hearts that these days there is no real danger that you are a spy, or a danger to the Mere.

While you are in the Star House, you may get a glimpse of the leaders of the town.

There are always 3 leaders, elected by the people of the town at the beginning of each year. The leaders wear heavy silver chains & long blue robes dotted with silver flecks. They pattern their faces with blue paint, according to ancient tradition, and do not cut their hair, which they curl into ringlets like the courtiers of the palace in Del.

Many people find them an awe-inspiring sight.

The Rithmere town leaders—an impressive sight

Places of Special Interest

❈ The **Rithmere Horse Stables** on the south side of town are where the most famous horses of the Mere are bred & trained. It is said that the great Adin was given his great white horse, Wing, during his visit to Rithmere.

If you are interested in horses, or wish to buy one, the stables are well worth a visit. Rithmere horses are handsome, fast, brave & long-lived & the stable masters are happy to bargain.

I am not tempted. I am more than happy with my faithful companion, Pearl.

❈ The **marketplace** is in the town center. All manner of goods are bought & sold. Only the Del marketplace can offer similar variety, but the marketplace of Rithmere is noisier & stranger, and the goods are not always what they seem. Be careful what you buy. There is no telling where it came from, or what it can do.

❈ The **inns**, like others in the land of the Lapis Lazuli, vary from pleasant retreats to dingy gambling dens. I recommend The Gamer's Retreat, The Rithmere Arms, The Moon & Stars & The Happy Wanderer, where at least the bedrooms have locks on the doors & the sheets are clean.

❈ The **racetrack** is at the southern edge of town, not far from the horse stables. Horses race there every day, fortunes are won & lost & many folk enjoy the color & bustle around the track & the food that is sold there.

❈ **The River Broad** is more sluggish here than it is further north, but it is still worth a visit. Fish throng it, partly because of the leftover food the Rithmere innkeepers throw into the water & the fishing is good. You can hire boats for fishing or pleasure if you wish. Ferries take passengers across the river for a small fee. The ferries are as flat as rafts, so can carry horses.

Note: Do not drink the river water without boiling it well first.

So, that is Rithmere. It has changed little since the last time I visited it years ago. Having done my duty by surveying it, I am comfortably settled now in a clean room in The Happy Wanderer, near the town's main gates. Having renewed my supplies, I will leave early tomorrow, heading for Emerald territory.

Main Roads Out of Rithmere

✦ The Rithmere Road runs north to join the Mountain Road.

✦ The Heavenly Way leads northwest, eventually splitting into 2, 1 track leading to Amethyst territory & the other to the territory of the Emerald.
   Note: Take plenty of water with you if you choose this path. There is little natural water in this part of the country.

✦ If you wish to return to Del, or go directly to Diamond territory, take a ferry across the River Broad & travel south by Adin's Ride, the road you will find on the other side. Adin's Ride eventually crosses Deltora Way. A signpost at the crossroads will direct you farther.
   I, of course, will be taking the Heavenly Way, the quickest path to Emerald territory. As I remember, it does not deserve its name, being narrow, rough & rutted with cart tracks. Perhaps it has improved since last I was here. We shall see . . .

10.

Emerald Territory

Wing backwards, burning
Dragon name.
Fang gnome-rest prey.
Each dragoneye aflame,
Read fiery smoke.

Emerald dragon fighting song

The Emerald Border

The Heavenly Way is just as rough as I remembered, but Pearl is a steady walker & we have made good time. I am now in Emerald territory, sitting with my back to a rock, brewing tea & having a welcome meal of bread & cheese before moving on.

Just before we crossed into Emerald territory, I saw the Lapis Lazuli dragon I spoke with in the Shifting Sands. She was flying from the direction of the Barrier Mountains, skimming along the border, keeping inside her own territory by a hair. When I asked her why she was taking this risk, she said she wanted to see if any Emerald dragons would come to warn her off. She was interested to see if the Emerald dragon tribe had fared better than her own.

I told her that her recklessness & curiosity would be her undoing, but she only laughed.

Emerald Dragons

Color: green.
Characteristics: stern, strong, proud, war-like, rigidly honorable, utterly dependable, little or no sense of humor.
Recent sighting: Lapis Lazuli border.
Food: Bubblers, Stingers, Blood Creepers, Ooze Toads & other cold-blooded denizens of the Barrier Mountains caves. (These are multiplying alarmingly as Emerald dragon numbers decline.) Also enjoy eels from the River Tor. Will, however, make do with warm-blooded creatures including humans, gnomes, Kin & horses if particularly hungry.

"I can outfly those lumbering Emerald beasts any day, Dragonfriend," she said. ("Dragonfriend" is the name I am called by all Deltora dragons. They would think it very bad taste to use my true name in casual conversation.)

"But see," she went on, "no Emerald dragon has come to challenge me, though I am sure my tail swayed across the borderline a few moments ago. Perhaps the stiff-necked beasts are all dead."

She sounded quite pleased at the thought, but her smile soon disappeared as, to my joy, a great green dragon came hurtling toward us from the north.

My Lapis Lazuli friend departed in some haste. I urged Pearl across the border & prepared to meet the newcomer.

Note: This is not something I would advise the ordinary traveler to do. On seeing a dragon approach you, you should either take shelter or remain quite still with your hands clearly visible. On no account draw your weapon.

The dragon of the Emerald recognized me & came to land. She was very stiff at first, because I had been talking to her enemy. But after formal greetings had been exchanged & I had explained that I had met the Lapis Lazuli dragon by chance, she unbent a little.

She told me, very reluctantly, that due to repeated Ak-Baba attacks over the past year only 3 dragons remained alive in Emerald territory.

"The Shadow beasts do not fight with honor," she said, curling her lip. "They attack in a pack & flee back across the Mountains when their filthy work is done."

Knowing in my heart that it was useless, I suggested that she & the other 2 surviving Emerald dragons should stay together. That way they could fight off enemy attack. As I expected, she immediately rejected the idea.

"Emerald dragons do not hunt in a *pack*," she said, pronouncing the word "pack" with disdain. "We have never done so & we will not begin now. Better to die with honor than to betray our traditions."

The Emerald dragon chases off the intruder

I opined that there was nothing dishonorable about banding together to fight for survival. But though she told me she knew I meant well, nothing I could say would make her change her mind & she soon took her leave, flying back the way she had come.

Emerald Territory—General Notes

❦ This is by far the bleakest and harshest territory in Deltora. I find its wildness bracing & refreshing to the spirit. Folk more used to comfortable living are usually happy to avoid it, especially in the winter.

❦ Except around the River Tor & close to the Barrier Mountains, natural water is scarce. Wild food is also scarce.
   Note: Do not travel far into Emerald territory without plentiful supplies or you may perish as others have done before you.

❦ By tradition Emerald territory is the land of the Dread Gnomes, 1 of Deltora's original 7 tribes. The gnomes, however, generally keep to their stronghold on Dread Mountain in the far northwest & do not trouble themselves about the rest of their domain.

❦ Much of the territory is deserted. The few small villages that exist are mostly in the south or by the River Tor. They have been populated by folk who have drifted into Emerald territory from other parts of Deltora, or from lands across the Silver Sea.

❦ Isolated farms & cottages are scattered throughout the territory. Their inhabitants are people who prefer to be alone. Some of these people will help a stranger in need. Others will not.

❦ Dangers in most of the territory are similar to those in other parts of Deltora, though there are fewer snakes here—perhaps it is too cold for them. The greatest & most unusual dangers occur close to the Barrier Mountains, so I will discuss them once I have moved north.

The Dreaming Spring

Pearl & I are spending this night beside Deltora's most mysterious spring, which lies not far from the border where I wrote my last notes.

The Dreaming Spring

The spring cannot be seen from the main road & few people know of it. It is at the end of a narrow track which branches off to the right. The track has no signpost but it is easily recognized for it is just past a tall pale gray rock shaped roughly like a man & known to the local people as "The Greer." ("Greers" were the half-humans used by the Shadow Lord to invade Deltora at the time of Adin.)

Note: The Dreaming Spring is enchanted. I have told you how to find it because it is 1 of the few sources of pure water in this part of the country. I do not like to think of travelers or their beasts dying of thirst while water is nearby. But it is vital that you consider the following warning before you drink.

The ancient brass plate fixed to 1 of the white stones that surround it bears the following message:

Drink, gentle stranger, & welcome.

All of evil will beware.

There is no doubt that folk who have wickedness in their hearts are in danger if they drink the water of the Dreaming Spring. If you regard this as ignorant superstition, you are sadly mistaken.

Strange, identical trees cluster around the spring. All of them have 3 branches stretching up from a smooth trunk. All have the same clusters of pale leaves.

Once these trees were living, breathing men & women who ignored the warning on the stone. I have been told this by the most truthful creatures alive—the Kin of Dread Mountain, who use the Dreaming Spring as their winter home.

Kin of old & present times have seen the following transformations:

*3 commanders in the Shadow Lord's invading army at the time of Adin.

*The leader of a murdering gang fleeing from justice in Rithmere.

*4 slave traders herding captives to the west coast for shipping across the Silver Sea.

*2 men who had robbed a nearby farm & burned it to the ground with the farmer unconscious inside it.

*A man & a woman who had come to the spring hoping to capture young Kin & sell them to the highest bidder.

The Kin know which tree each of these people became. They cannot identify the other trees in the grove. Presumably those transformations occurred in the summer months when the Kin had returned to Dread Mountain.

When I last came to the Dreaming Spring there were 35 trees around it. Today I counted 37. Sometime in the last 5 years, 2 more evildoers have ignored the warning sign & met a terrible fate.

Is It Safe to Drink from the Dreaming Spring?

I cannot tell you. All I can say is that I believe the spring punishes only cold wickedness, and forgives ordinary human faults.

I myself am prone to anger, impatience, pride & selfishness. I am not gentle or tenderhearted. I have often wished folk ill (especially when I am condemned to stay in the palace in Del for more than a few days!). Yet I have drunk the water safely many times & have done so again tonight.

Only you know the secrets of your own heart. You must decide for yourself if the risk is worth taking.

The Second Power of the Spring

The second mysterious power of the Dreaming Spring is the power that gives it its name.

The water will make you sleep heavily & whatever or whoever you picture in your mind as you drink, you will visit in spirit. Not in the ordinary way of dreams, but in reality.

If you think of a particular person as you drink, for example, you will later visit that person while you sleep. Folk you visit in this way will not be able to see or hear you & will be quite unaware of your presence, but you will be with them as surely as if you were standing beside them in bodily form.

This can be a great comfort for those who see their loved ones safe & well. For those who see otherwise it can be anguish, as I know only too well.

I should add that the water of the Dreaming Spring does not allow you to visit the dead. I have tried it.

Shadowgate

Since leaving the Dreaming Spring I have traveled for some days without much pause. I carried some of the magic water away with me & used a little of it to try to locate the other 2 Emerald dragons. I regret to tell you that I failed. It seems that the Emerald dragon I spoke to at the Lapis Lazuli border has become her great tribe's only survivor. May she keep safe! I now take up my pen in the village of Shadowgate, far to the north.

I have found a bed in Shadowgate's only tavern. The tavern has no official name but is usually called "Greasy's Place." "Greasy" is no longer the landlord, having been dead for 30 years, but he was a great character, it seems & the name has stuck. The tavern's present owner, a wiry little woman called Janet, seems not to mind. Her only concern is that folk pay promptly for what they eat & drink under her roof & refrain from fighting in the bar.

Shadowgate is 1 of Emerald territory's few northern villages. By my reckoning it is the most northerly place in Deltora. It huddles in the foothills of the Barrier Mountains & is surrounded by the bleakest country imaginable.

A signpost on the Mountain Road points to the Shadowgate track. The track leads through a rocky pass, which can be extremely dangerous due to falling rocks & the creatures that lurk in & around it.

Move through the pass as quickly as you can. Do not stop to investigate anything you see.

A high fence of straight, pointed sticks surrounds the village. Stone is more plentiful than wood in the area & when I first came upon Shadowgate years ago I asked why the barrier had not been built of stones. The people told me that the beasts & human predators that prowl the foothills find sticks difficult to climb. A wall of stone would provide too many footholds. The fence does have deep stone foundations, however, to stop beasts from tunneling underneath it.

Shadowgate Village

Why Visit Shadowgate?

Life in Shadowgate is harsh. There are few luxuries to be had & dangers are everywhere. Perhaps you wonder, then, why I have chosen to come here instead of moving directly to Dread Mountain.

First, Shadowgate is one of the very few places in the north where a traveler can be certain of being able to buy fresh supplies of food & medicine.

Second, the people of Shadowgate are well worth meeting. Folk here are practical, determined & courageous

& learn sturdy independence from a very early age. They work hard, but know how to enjoy themselves. Isolated as they are, they joyously welcome any traveler, peddler or wandering entertainer who happens to come their way.

In addition, they are among the few Deltorans who understand the importance of dragons. They rejoice to see dragons in their skies, because they know the dragons hunt the dangerous creatures that surround their village.

This brings me to the last reason for visiting Shadowgate. It gives the traveler the chance to see at first hand some of the ghastly but fascinating beasts of the Barrier Mountains.

Some Monsters of the Mountains

Legend has it that a great eruption of the seabed in ancient times caused the Barrier Mountains to form. It is also said that many of the denizens of the Mountains are sea creatures that have adapted to life on land.

My observations of some of the beasts around Shadowgate have led me to believe that these legends are based on truth.

The creatures I list below are probably not unique to the Shadowgate area. No doubt they exist all through the Barrier Mountains. But Shadowgate is the only Deltoran village to lie in the Mountains' foothills. It provides the least dangerous base for the adventurer wanting to learn more about the Mountains & their dangers.

Bubblers

These pale, toothless, boneless creatures, which look rather like large sea cucumbers, live in large colonies deep within cliffs & rocks. A large colony lives in the rock walls of the pass that leads into Shadowgate.

Bubblers have weak eyesight, but their sense of smell is very strong. When they sense warm, living flesh nearby, they begin exuding thick, frothing white slime. The slime greases the rock, allowing the Bubblers to squeeze out of the narrowest cracks & holes to attack their prey.

They generally attack in huge numbers, eventually swarming over the victim's head & killing by suffocation. They then produce more frothing slime, which eventually dissolves their prey's flesh so it can be easily absorbed.

Note 1: Be on the watch for white froth appearing on the surface of rocks & cliffs. The froth is a sign that Bubblers are preparing to attack. Leave the area immediately.

Note 2: Should you be overtaken, fire is your best defense. If you are daubed with slime, remove the mess as quickly as possible using a cloth soaked in oil. The slime is waterproof, so cannot be washed off.

Stingers

The dome-shaped bodies of these beasts look amazingly like the bodies of the stinging jellyfish I have seen in the

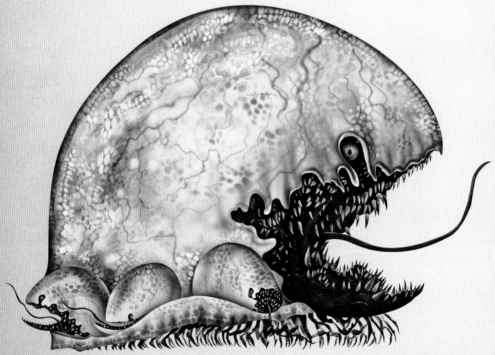

Stinger

waters around Broome. Stingers, however, breathe air, have visible eyes & mouths & are monstrous. The largest I have seen was the size of a typical kitchen table, but the people of Shadowgate tell me that deep within the Mountains, where dragons do not hunt, Stingers can grow as big as houses.

Stingers have hundreds of tiny legs that are almost hidden beneath the skirts of skin that hang from their bulbous bodies. They capture their victims as frogs capture flies, their long tongues flicking from their mouths with deadly speed.

Occasionally a Stinger may be seen carrying its young in the pouches that edge its dome. The first Stinger I ever saw was carrying 4 young in this way & at first I thought it had 5 heads! The young have long tongues just as the parent Stinger does, so a Stinger with young is even more dangerous than a Stinger without.

Sword cuts will do little more than enrage an attacking Stinger. If you are trapped, fire is your best defense. But the best thing to do on seeing a Stinger, even in the distance, is to take to your heels & run for your life.

Blood Creepers

Blood Creepers are so called because they are scarlet in color, leave a slime trail that resembles blood & are attracted by the smell of blood. They look like large crabs. However, except for their tearing pincers, which are very hard, their shells are much softer than crabs' shells. They live under rocks or in holes in the ground.

Blood Creepers are usually scavengers, eating the remains of dead animals, but they will also attack any creature or human made helpless by injury, unconsciousness or sleep.

While visiting Shadowgate, never be tempted to sleep or even doze outside the village wall. Blood Creepers can strip flesh from a bone in moments & more Creepers will come with every drop of blood spilled.

Blood Creeper and victim

Ooze Toads

Ooze Toads both sweat & spit venom so powerful that it kills on contact. Dragons seem to be the only creatures that are immune to this venom.

Ooze Toads are extremely aggressive & will spit at anything that moves. Fortunately, they are rare. They always live alone & prefer damp, dark caverns underground, but young ones are sometimes found in caves or rocky hollows on the surface, so they are worth mentioning here.

The usual snakebite cure is not effective against Ooze Toad venom. It is said that the great Adin once saved his horse Wing from death by washing away an Ooze Toad's venom & pressing the great Ruby talisman of the Ralad people against the place the venom had touched. This may be truth or legend, but either way it is of little use to the ordinary traveler.

It is said that these creatures can live for centuries & never stop growing. Years ago I saw a dragon catch a toad

Ooze Toad

that was as big as a calf. It is quite possible that 1 or 2 truly monstrous Ooze Toads lie hidden in lairs deep within the Mountains. One can only hope they stay there.

Bandit Gangs

I include these men & women among the monsters of the Mountains because in my view they are monstrous indeed. Tales of their cowardly cruelty & evil ways abound in Emerald territory & indeed in the other territories that border the Barrier Mountains.

Most are desperate criminals who took refuge in the Mountains when being pursued by the law. Others are simple runaways who thought to escape harsh parents or

masters, or the memories of sad love affairs, by hiding
themselves in a place where no one would seek them.
A few are folk who foolishly wandered deep into the
Mountains & became lost. But no matter how they came to
the Mountains, all who survive & remain seem to become
corrupted. It is as if some evil power takes hold of their
minds & seeps into their very bones.

The sorcerer who rules the land beyond the Mountains
is the source of this evil, I am sure of it. Emerald dragons
have told me that in olden times he had a den hidden
deep among the peaks of the west. They believe that the
Mountains are still under his influence to this day, but
they can do nothing to remedy this, for the Mountains are
not their territory.

Only Dread Mountain, the domain of the Dread
Gnomes, is the exception to this rule. And now that I have
replenished my supplies it is to Dread Mountain that I
will go next.

———————◦»○◦———————

Dread Mountain

The Mountain Road will take you directly to Dread
Mountain. It is quite safe to camp along the way, provided
you take the usual precautions. The road follows the line
of the Mountains but keeps a safe distance from them, so
Blood Creepers & the like should not trouble you.

I strongly advise you not to attempt to climb Dread
Mountain in winter. The cold is bitter & paths are covered
in snow. At other times of the year, a pleasant couple of
days may be spent on the mountainside.

A rough track leads up Dread Mountain on its western
face. This is the path I have taken & the only path you
should attempt to follow. All other ways end in cliffs,
chasms or thickets of Boolong trees that will cut you to
ribbons if you try to push through them.

I have climbed, leading Pearl, for almost 2 hours

& as the sun is setting I have decided to stop for the night. The streams of Dread Mountain are crystal clear. I am sitting beside a stream at present, eating dried fruit & travelers' biscuit. Water will be my only drink tonight, because I would not dare to light a fire amid such thick forest.

In the distance I can hear Kin talking as they eat their last Boolong cones for the day. I will not disturb them now, but will seek them out in the morning. I will occupy my time before sleep this night by making notes in this journal. I have realized that there is much to say about safe traveling on Dread Mountain.

The Dread Gnomes

In the days before Adin, the Dread Gnomes killed intruders without hesitation. Adin dared to climb the Mountain, however & eventually won the gnomes' loyalty. Since that time, visitors no longer have to fear the Dread Gnomes' arrows—if they take certain precautions.

1. Do not climb higher than halfway up the Mountain. The gnomes' stronghold—an underground maze of rooms & tunnels—is at the Mountain's peak. The stronghold is filled with treasure & the gnomes will defend it ferociously. A sign of crossed arrows on the main path will tell you when you have climbed high enough & should turn back.

2. Many small paths run from the main track all the way up the Mountain. Follow these paths by all means, but do not enter any huts you may find along the way. These huts, always marked with the sign of the crossed arrows, are gnome rests. They have been built as refuges for gnomes in the case of storms & high winds & are forbidden to strangers.

Every gnome rest has a gnomish name. Today I passed TONOD, TIEKAT, FFO, REVETAHW, MMURD & SYAS.

3. If you meet a group of gnomes while climbing the Mountain, bow low & state your name & business ("traveler in Deltora"). If you are asked to do so,

drop your weapons & raise your hands.

There will be nothing to fear if you follow these instructions. Dread Gnomes are suspicious folk, but honorable. They will not kill unless they suspect treachery. Do not expect them to invite you to their stronghold, however. They are excellent hosts when friends visit, but they are wary of strangers. It has taken me many years to win their trust.

Drop your weapons &
raise your hands

Other Dangers of Dread Mountain

❧ **Boolong Trees.** These stubby evergreen trees grow all over the Mountain. Their wickedly thorny leaves block shortcuts & cause both gnomes & travelers to keep to the well-beaten paths. If it were not for the Kin, who eat the leaves & the small black cones of the Boolongs, thus keeping the trees in some control, it would be almost impossible to move on the Mountain at all.

❧ **Green Beasts.** Because it is so close to the Shadowlands border, Dread Mountain is sometimes invaded by the giant Shadowlands lizards known as "Green Beasts." The Dread Gnomes have successfully rid their Mountain of all other dangerous pests, but Green Beasts remain a problem.

Green Beasts are taller than a man, have terrible teeth & claws & are vicious fighters. Their hide is as strong as armor. Fortunately they are not particularly intelligent & have 1 weak place—the underside of the throat is soft & can be pierced by sword, spear or heavy-headed arrow.

Green Beasts: Aim for the throat

❧ **Red Moss.** You will find pads of this moss floating in Dread Mountain streams. Do not touch it. It burns the skin. If you are surprised by a Green Beast, however, pick up some Red Moss with a gloved hand & hurl it at the beast, aiming for throat or eyes. The moss will sting & burn the lizard, giving you a chance to flee.

Note: Strangely enough, in its green form (that is, when alive & growing on stream banks) the moss is very good for healing wounds.

The Kin

These gentle, intelligent flying beings spend their springs, summers & autumns on Dread Mountain & their winters at the Dreaming Spring (discussed earlier).

Kin are very appealing to look at, with large, dark eyes, dense fur like brown moss & plump bodies supported on short legs. They stand upright & walk with a rolling motion. Their velvety wings are kept closely folded when the Kin are not in flight. Female Kin have pouches in which they carry their young.

Though few people have actually seen a Kin for themselves, tales of them have spread throughout Deltora. It is common for young Deltoran children to have soft toys shaped like Kin.

It is quite wrong to think of the Kin as merely appealing animals, however. Kin can speak & reason as well as any gnome or human—& far better than many I could name. They have a leader, usually the oldest member of the tribe, but they always discuss important matters as a group, in a civilized fashion.

Their needs are simple. On Dread Mountain they eat the cones & leaves of Boolong trees & at the Dreaming Spring they eat grass. They drink only water. They require no shelter because they sleep curled into a tight ball & their fur repels the rain. A sleeping Kin looks so like a rock that it is possible to pass it by without noticing it.

Kin are peaceful & usually prefer to retreat from danger, but they will defend themselves if necessary. On Dread Mountain they use Red Moss against Green Beasts with great effect.

The Dread Gnomes will kill Kin if they can, as garments made from Kin skin are highly prized, being rainproof, protective & hard-wearing. Fortunately, however, thickets of Boolong trees usually provide a safe refuge from gnome hunters. In any case, the gnomes' arrows are too small to do a great deal of damage to Kin adults & tender young are always kept safely in their mothers' pouches.

Kin are generally shy & keep to themselves. You will be lucky to meet with them. If you do, you only need to be friendly & polite & you will surely be treated with equal kindness.

Leaving Dread Mountain

Tonight is my 3rd night on Dread Mountain. I have rested well, spent happy hours talking to the Kin & feasted with the Dread Gnomes. Happily I have seen no Green Beasts. Thanks to the water from the Dreaming Spring I know that the last Emerald dragon is still safe & taking care to remain so, though it goes against her nature to hide from her enemies instead of fighting.

To leave Dread Mountain, follow the stream that flows down the Mountain's western face & you will at last reach the River Tor. The Tor will guide you south into Amethyst territory, as well as leading you to the quickest route back to Del, if this is what you wish.

In many ways I would like to return to Del at once. But for several reasons I must continue my journey. Tomorrow, all being well, I will be in Amethyst territory.

11.

Amethyst Territory

Stones burn telling
Dragon fortune,
Surrounding fiery border
On mirror dragons use.

Amethyst dragon song

I write these notes by lantern light, beside the River Tor in the north of Amethyst territory. It is some days since I opened this journal. I have not had the heart for writing. Tonight, however, I am determined to make up for lost time.

The land of the Amethyst is the territory of the Toran people, who are strong in magic & can read each other's thoughts. It is said also that the Torans can tell the future by means of fortune-telling stones.

The Torans live in the white city of Tora, which lies beside the river downstream from here. You rarely see Torans outside their city's walls, though their leaders do sometimes visit Del to meet with the king. Deltora Way was built to make travel between the 2 great cities faster & easier. Sped by magic, Torans can make the long journey to Del in hours.

The rest of Amethyst territory has been settled by folk from other parts of Deltora or from across the sea. The Torans usually take little notice of these settlers. If

Amethyst Dragons

Color: purple.
Characteristics: wise, truthful, philosophical, responsible. Enjoy intelligent discussion & poetry. The longest-lived & largest of all Deltoran dragons.
Recent sighting: where the River Tor meets the sea.
Food: fish of the Silver Sea, Tor eels, seaweed (all varieties).

they sense evil or danger, however, they can unite their wills to drive unwelcome visitors out. This makes the land of the Amethyst the safest & most peaceful of all the 7 territories.

Del palace courtiers think that Tora is the only place worth visiting in the west, because Tora is a great city, created by magic & famous for its luxury & elegance.

As you might expect, I do not agree. I have often visited the Amethyst north without setting foot in Tora. Yet I never fail to visit the coast, to relish its wild beauty & share a meal with the keeper of the famous Bone Point lighthouse.

I need to speak to the Toran leaders urgently, however, so I have decided to go downriver to the white city without delay. I am sure that few readers of this book will object to this plan. Having reached Amethyst territory, most travelers cannot wait to see Tora.

The River Tor

❦ The Tor rises in Emerald territory & flows into the land of the Amethyst. Just above Tora it is joined by the River Broad, which has become a narrower stream after its long journey from the land of the Opal. The Tor then widens and runs on to the Silver Sea.

❦ The Tor is the most beautiful river in Deltora, being deep, fast-moving, crystal clear & thronged with waterbirds. It is pleasant to walk or ride along its shaded banks & the fishing is good. There are many excellent riverbank camping spots where a traveler may spend the night in comfort, as I am doing at this moment.

❦ Boats large & small ply the river. Some of these are paddle steamers that carry passengers. Simply wait on 1 of the marked public jetties strung all along the stream & soon enough a boat will be along to pick you up. Traveling by water is always enjoyable, but as I have Pearl with me I cannot do it this time. Passenger boats will not carry horses.

Note: It is best to avoid boats that use 1 or more of the creatures called Polypans* as crew. Such boats are not always reliable.

❋ There are many small villages on both sides of the river where you may buy a simple meal & even a bed for the night, if you wish. The river folk are friendly to strangers & will be interested in any news you have to tell them, particularly of Del.

❋ Three bridges cross the Tor. King's Bridge, not far downstream from Tora, was Ralad-built by order of King Brandon, so it is good & sturdy. The other 2 are merely narrow swinging rope & plank constructions, unsuitable for horses or carts. They are in bad repair & in my view quite unsafe. The local people use them sometimes, but I would advise you not to, especially if you are a weak swimmer.

❋ It used to be common to see Amethyst dragons above the river, hunting fish & eels, but as yet I have seen no dragons at all.

There—I have done my duty. Now I can sleep.

The River Tor, with rope & plank bridge in foreground

*Polypans

Polypans are hairy, ape-like beings sometimes used as crew on Tor riverboats. They are not native to Deltora. Most have arrived on ships from foreign ports & have either been sold to Deltorans on the west coast or have simply deserted their ships to seek their fortunes elsewhere.

Though not much taller than a 10-year-old child, Polypans are immensely strong. They cannot speak, but can understand simple instructions.

Polypans can be loyal & loving companions for lonely people who treat them well. Unfortunately most of the Polypans used on ships & boats are not treated kindly. They are valued only because they are strong, will do the roughest, dirtiest & hardest work & do not ask for pay. All they require is food & a plentiful supply of the evil-smelling chewing toffee to which almost all of them have become addicted while young.

While it suits them, riverboat Polypans will work hard, but they will not hesitate to abandon their boat & its passengers at the first sign of danger, or if their supply of chewing toffee fails. It is dangerous & irresponsible to use them in place of human crew.

Note: Some riverboat captains also value Polypans because they are expert pickpockets who can steal passengers' purses & jewelry without being noticed.

Polypan

Where Waters Meet

You will know you are less than a day from Tora when you reach the place where the River Broad flows into the Tor.

A good bridge, with a high arch to allow boats to pass under it, crosses the Broad here. It is called Zara's Bridge in honor of the Toran bride of the great Adin. Cross the bridge & you will find yourself in the busy village of Where Waters Meet. You should buy more traveling supplies here, if you need them. You will not be able to do this in Tora.

I always enjoy visiting Where Waters Meet. When I reached it this afternoon I decided to stop & spend the night rather than pressing on to Tora at once. Pearl needs rest & I want to be fresh for my meeting with the Toran leaders.

There is only 1 inn in the village. It is called The Jumping Fish & I can heartily recommend it. The rooms are clean & the food is excellent—even the cooks of Hira could not produce a better fish pie.

Vegetable gardens surround Where Waters Meet & the people keep cows, pigs, sheep, chickens & ducks. The river provides fish & eels. But the village thrives mainly because of its position. The paddle steamers of the 2 rivers stop here to buy fresh food & other goods. While the crews see to this, passengers always get off the boat to stretch their legs & look around. The village shops & stalls, not to mention the tavern, do very good business selling food, drink & souvenirs such as carved waterbirds & knitted dolls to the visitors.

The folk I have spoken to here have not seen an Amethyst dragon for some weeks. They are pleased about this because without dragons hunting over the river there are all the more fish for them to catch. I did not argue with them. They are good people—only unthinking.

Well, there is no point in brooding uselessly. It is time to put out my candle & sleep. Tomorrow—Tora.

The City of Tora

I reached Tora this morning. I had meant to stay a few hours at most, but now it is night & I am still here. My meeting with the Toran leaders took longer than I had expected. By the time we had finished, the sun was setting & they asked me to stay the night.

I could not refuse their kind invitation, though they had disappointed me. Anger is impossible in Tora, for reasons I will explain later.

So I write these notes in a silent, white, Toran guest room, instead of by a campfire on the riverbank downstream as I had intended.

The city of Tora

It is said that Tora was carved by magic from a marble
mountain & that it is all of a piece, without crack or
seam. It stands at the edge of a lake that separates it
from the main stream of the River Tor. It is a city of
light, flowers & sparkling fountains. Everything in it is
controlled by magic—even the weather. Tora is totally
self-sufficient. Magic supplies its food, its drink & its
many comforts. It is a very beautiful place—if cold,
perfect, isolated splendor is to your taste.

Entering Tora: The Magic Archway

Tora has no city gate. Its only entrance is a large archway
that appears totally unguarded. In fact, the archway itself
protects the city.

The archway is so deep that it forms a short tunnel.
When you move into this echoing space, you will feel a
cold tingling all over your body. At the same moment,
sparks of colored light will swirl around you. You will
not be able to see these sparks. They are only visible to
people watching from outside the city.

The archway's magic draws all evil from the person
who enters it. Strong emotions & negative feelings such as
bitterness, anger & despair also drain away. This effect is
so powerful that the truly wicked are forced to retreat,
weakened & almost emptied of life. Lesser criminals may
go on, but by the time they reach the city they have lost
their desire to do harm.

Ordinary beings like myself (& most of my readers, I
daresay) feel merely soothed by the magic of the archway.
If you are a naturally fiery person you will feel a little
unlike yourself during your stay in Tora. But do not
fear—once you have left the city you will return to
normal quite quickly.

Toran Ways & Manners

◄ Torans are tall & slender. Men & women both have
straight black hair that hangs almost to their waists &

is as fine as silk. They wear long, fine robes in many different colors. They are calm, intelligent people who always think logically & are never hot or impetuous. If they have a fault, it is that they are as self-contained as the city that provides for their every need. They can appear cold & unemotional to ordinary folk.

❦ On arrival in Tora you will be greeted with grave politeness. Thereafter you will be treated as an honored guest. You will not be expected to pay for food, drink or shelter.
Note: It is considered impolite to offer payment.

❦ Make the most of your time in the city, for it will be short. Visitors are expected to stay for 1 night only. Sometimes the Torans will invite you to stay longer, but such invitations are very rare.

❦ There are no shops or stalls in Tora. There is nothing to buy, for nothing in Tora is for sale. This rule is unbreakable.

❦ Feel free to wander anywhere you wish in the city. If the Torans do not want you to enter a particular place, you will find you cannot enter it, though the doors may stand wide open.

❦ Torans weave with great skill. Their homes & halls are filled with glorious fabrics made by their own hands & some of these fabrics shimmer with magic. You may feast your eyes on them but it is pointless to try to touch or buy them.

❦ Do not bother stuffing your pockets with the delicious free food that loads the dining tables. Toran food & drink vanishes if taken out of the city. This is why I always renew my supplies at Where Waters Meet.

❦ Do not ask to see or use the fortune-telling stones. They are strictly for Toran use only.

The Oath Stone

All roads in Tora lead to a large square at the city's heart.
Before the time of Adin, the great Amethyst that was the
Toran talisman lay on a marble table in the center of this
square. Now, where the table once stood, there is a huge
marble slab flickering with cold green fire. This is the
oath stone & its magic is so powerful that you will feel it
tingling on your skin the moment you enter the square.

The Toran Oath Stone

These words are engraved on the stone:

We, the people of Tora, swear loyalty to Adin, King of Deltora & all of his blood who follow him. If ever this vow is broken, may this rock, our city's heart, break also & may we be swept away, forever to regret our dishonor.

All the 7 tribes swore loyalty to Adin. But only the Torans felt the need to bind their descendants to their oath so powerfully that to break it would mean their destruction. Why was this so?

I suspect that the proud tribe of Tora felt shame because at first it refused to allow its talisman to join the other gems in the magic Belt of Deltora. Tora was protected from all evil & the fate of others in the land did not seem important to the Torans of those days. Only at the last, desperate hour, when all seemed lost, did Tora at last change its mind so that the battle with the Shadow Lord could be won.

The Torans of today do not like to remember this, as I discovered when I talked of it this afternoon. They find their ancestors' selfishness embarrassing and want it to be forgotten. But, as I told them, if we forget our mistakes we are in danger of repeating them.

Toran Fortune-telling Stones

The 40 fortune-telling stones are small oval river stones, each marked with a different symbol. They have existed since the days when Torans lived in huts of grass & branches & the great white city by the lake had not been thought of.

To tell the future, or to help the tribe make a decision, a Toran leader, with eyes closed, puts his or her hand into the ancient woven bag in which the stones are kept. The leader gathers up 9 stones & casts them gently upon the ground. All the leaders together then try to decide what the stones are telling them. This is not a simple matter, as most of the symbols have several different meanings. The pattern in which the stones fall is also believed to be important.

I cannot tell you the symbols on all the stones. I can only tell you the symbols on the 9 stones that I saw cast this afternoon.

We had discussed the slaughter of the dragons. Like the Ralad folk, the Torans regret it keenly. Sadly, they told me, their banishing spells have no effect on creatures that fly as high as the Ak-Baba. They cannot protect their skies.

I had suspected this. And in any case, I was not concerned just with Amethyst territory, but with the whole of Deltora. I had another request for them. I wanted them to use their influence to gain a meeting with King Lucan & talk to him about the dragons on my behalf.

They were unwilling. They had only recently visited King Lucan in Del & had mentioned the Ak-Baba attacks then. The king did not seem to think there was any harm in what was happening. He said that a slight drop in the number of dragons would be a good thing for the people, who were afraid of them. Chief Advisor Drumm was with him, nodding & agreeing all the while.

The Torans felt that their oath of loyalty forbade them from troubling the king further on the matter. They had been grieved to find that he was failing in health. When they saw him he was pale & trembling, they said—looking far older than his years & clearly not fit for travel.

This news surprised me greatly. I knew King Lucan had been a little unwell while I was away at sea, but I had no idea his illness had persisted & become so severe.

I had treasured great hopes of my Toran visit. I admit that for a moment, despite the city's calming effect, I was so shocked & disappointed that I did not know what to say.

To comfort me & perhaps to reassure themselves, the Torans cast the fortune-telling stones. This is how the stones fell:

water, the river or a wanderer	*cloud, evil, danger or an error*	*death, sleep or an ending*
a dwelling, safety or trust	*dragon, the land, all living things*	*a secret, a plot or something hidden*
the moon, time, patience or mystery	*hope, action, a young leader or king*	*star, birth, rebirth or a new beginning*

136

This is how the Torans read the stones:

*The wanderer (Doran) is in error.
*The dragons are threatened with death, but we can trust
that they will be safe.
*In time, a secret will be revealed & a young king will be
the cause of a new beginning.

The Torans also pointed out that the stone bearing the
symbol of Tora was absent.

They concluded from all this that the dragons will
survive without their help & the problem will be solved
in the reign of King Lucan's son, Gareth. We have only to
trust & be patient.

I was not reassured. I think there is another way to
read the stones—perhaps several other ways. I feel the
stones were sending a strong message to me—& it was
not that I should be patient. By the time Gareth becomes
king it will be too late for the last dragons to be saved.
Something must be done at once—but what?

I do not like the stone meaning "a secret, a plot or
something hidden." I sense that the cloud covering the
wanderer does not mean "error," but "danger."

Well, if I am in danger, so be it. I must think about
the stones' message in the days to come. I must make
a plan. The Torans will not help. I now know that the
dragons' survival is up to me.

Before I sleep I will take a sip of dreaming water &
think of the Amethyst dragon I know best. I pray I will
see him in my dreams.

———⟫●⟨———

The Amethyst Coast

I am now on the coast—at the long stretch of sand where the River Tor meets the Silver Sea. To my right is the broad channel dug by the Tor as it rushes to meet the waves. Beyond the channel is a headland, at its base the flat sheet of rock beneath which is the monster's lair known as the Maze of the Beast. To my left is Dead Man's Rock, a headland pitted with caves & shaped like a skull. The Amethyst dragon I know best is catching fish beyond the breaking waves as the sun dips below the horizon.

The dragon was here on my arrival & my joy at finding him alive & well was very great. He was equally overjoyed to see me, but the news he had to tell me was grave.

He is the last of his tribe—all the rest are dead. "And I will soon be joining them," he told me. "So far I have survived by hiding here on the shore, but the Shadow beasts will hunt me down in the end. There is no help for it."

Dead Man's Rock

I said I would not accept that. I said he *must* survive.
There *must* be a way. I showed him my sketch of the Toran
fortune-telling stones & after that we talked for hours.

We decided many things. The first was that I must
fulfill my duty to finish this book. It will gain me nothing
to earn the disapproval of the king.

So here are some notes on the Amethyst coast. The
whole coast is magnificent & filled with interest because of
the many trading ships that visit from across the Silver
Sea. There are certain places, however, that should be
especially noted.

The Bone Point Lighthouse

The lonely lighthouse at
Bone Point in the north
was built by order of
the great Adin to stop
ships coming to grief on
the wicked Bone Point
rocks. The lighthouse
is a miracle of Ralad
building & is protected
from attack & decay by
Toran magic. I have not
seen it for a couple of
years, but the dragon
tells me it is still as
perfect as the day it
was built. To reach it,
cross the King's Bridge
downriver from Tora &
follow the Bone Point
Road. The present
keeper of the light, Ulay
Bran, will welcome you
heartily & show you
around.

Bone Point Lighthouse

139

The Maze of the Beast

Anyone who travels to Amethyst territory will soon hear of the Maze of the Beast. So many wild, dark stories are whispered about this place that a traveler might be forgiven for thinking that it is merely a legend, with no real existence.

But the Maze of the Beast does exist. l have seen it. And l have glimpsed the ancient & fearsome creature that inhabits it—the monstrous, pale slug-like creature called the Death Spinner or the Glus.

The Glus

The Maze is a series of partly flooded white caverns hidden beneath a sheet of flat rock & the sea. lt is at the base of the headland to the right of where l am sitting writing these words now.

It is said that for centuries the Glus has been sliding through the dimness of the Maze, enlarging it & mending the walls with sticky white threads it sprays from its mouth. It is interesting to note that the beast uses these same white threads to catch & bind any creature that falls or blunders into the Maze, so it can feed on its prey at its leisure.

If you wish to see the Glus for yourself, you must cross the King's Bridge & continue down to the coast on the western side of the river.

When you have reached the sands, wait until low tide & walk around the headland, keeping close to the cliff to avoid the danger of the Maze blowhole.* You will soon see a huge cavern that is open to the sea. Only at low tide can you edge into this cavern & move onto the great slab of rock that hangs above the waterline.

On the right-hand side of the rock slab (as you face the back of the cavern) you will see a dark hole. This is the largest entrance to the Maze of the Beast & if it is as I left it last time I visited, it will be covered by a steel grating bolted to the rock.

If the grating is missing, keep away from the hole. If the grating is secure, drop a pebble through it & wait. Soon you will hear the rippling of water & a stealthy, sliding sound. Then you will see the pale shape of the Glus below, sliding to the place where the pebble has fallen, expecting to find prey.

Note: Stay well back. The white threads gush from the Glus's mouth like arrows flying from a bow. The threads are very sticky & very strong. I cannot guarantee that if they catch you, they might not pull you down into the depths of the Maze despite the grating. It is up to you to take care.

The Maze Blowhole

The sheet of rock that covers much of the Maze of the Beast can be dangerous to walk upon. Every now and then a spout of water gushes high into the air from a hole in the rock.

This is the Maze Blowhole & is an amazing sight. It is also perilous for those foolish enough to walk or run near it when it is about to blow. The force of the water is quite enough to overbalance a grown man, who may then be sucked back into the hole to drown.

Some folk will tell you that the gush of water is produced by the Glus, but this is not true. The blowhole is a natural spout of air & water caused by the shape of the rock & the pressure of the tide.

The Dreaming Dunes

We have now moved farther south & have reached the Dreaming Dunes, which has always been 1 of my favorite places in the west. It is a gloriously peaceful beach where the waves lap gently & row after row of sand dunes ripple back toward the horizon. The dragon of the Amethyst is still with us. Pearl has grown used to his company & no longer fears him. She even watched with interest, rather than anxiety, as the dragon took me high over the sea as the sun set.

Tonight we will camp together on the dunes. Tomorrow Pearl & I will move on along the Coast Road to Diamond territory. I want to complete this journey as fast as possible and deliver my book, so I can set out again to carry out the idea that the fortune-telling stones have given me.

Despite my fears & troubles, I am strangely happy. Truly there is no greater joy than flying with dragons.

12.

Diamond Territory

Fiery dragon
Sentences three prey.
Last in talons burn fanged word.
Fourth blazes every scale.

Diamond dragon fighting song

Diamond Territory is the land of the war-like Jalis, famous for their love of battle & the golden armor worn by their knights.

Before the time of Adin, the Jalis killed intruders into their territory without hesitation. This is no longer the case, though it is wise for visitors to behave well & courteously at all times. No Jalis will forgive an insult, or turn away from the chance to fight.

When not on duty patrolling their territory's borders, Jalis knights live in or near the city of Jaliad & spend most of their time training & staging mock battles. Jalis in other parts of the territory make their living in the ordinary way as fisherfolk, farmers, shopkeepers & tradespeople. These Jalis may not wear the golden armor, but they are just as quick to take offense as the knights & are just as ready to fight, so must be treated with respect.

Diamond Dragons

Color: sometimes described as silver, but in fact scales are colorless, flashing silver-blue in light.
Characteristics: aggressive & ruthless when dealing with enemies, supremely loyal & generous to friends. Superstitious. Great respecters of tradition. The strongest of all Deltoran dragons, traditionally hunted by Jalis knights as proof of valor.
Recent sighting: Blood Lily Island.
Food: sea creatures such as large fish, Kobb young, sea serpents & Bird Banes. On land, Diamond Pythons, Tuskers, occasional domestic animals. Will graze on Blood Lilies & Grippers.

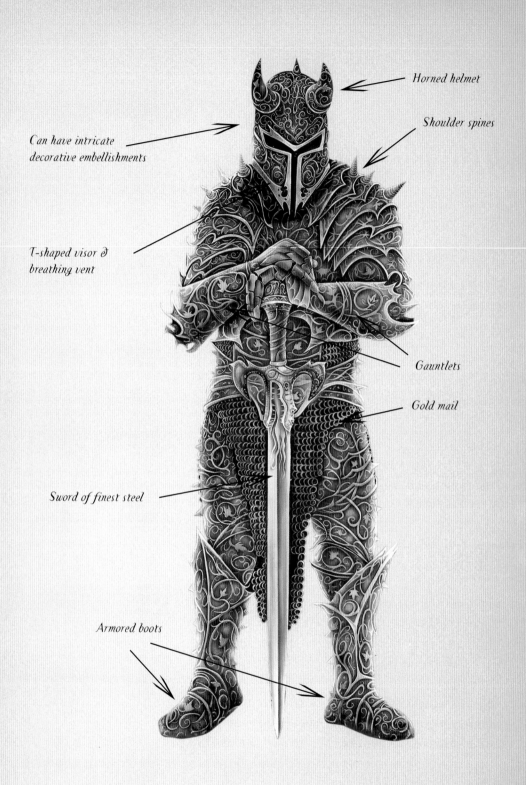

Horned helmet

Shoulder spines

Can have intricate
decorative embellishments

T-shaped visor &
breathing vent

Gauntlets

Gold mail

Sword of finest steel

Armored boots

The distinctive golden battle armor of the Jalis knight

The Finger

An hour ago Pearl & I reached The Finger, a long, narrow spar
of flat rock that stretches into the sea at the most western point
of Diamond territory, with 2 islands at its tip.

Here the Silver Sea meets the Ocean of the South. It is a
wild & beautiful place—one of my favorite places in the whole
of Deltora.

A small, rounded building has always stood on The Finger,
but it does not spoil the view. It is so low & brown that it looks
as if it has grown out of the rock itself. The local people say
that it has had various uses over the centuries, but during my
time it has always been Milly's Chowder House.

I am sitting in the Chowder House now. It is dim & smoky,
filled with the fumes of simmering chowder (a kind of fish stew)
& the fish oil that fuels its lanterns. But the chowder is more
delicious than anything I have ever tasted, especially sopped up
with a crust of Milly's new-baked bread.

Today I have the Chowder House to myself, but I have seen
it filled to bursting & shaking with noise. Foreign ships often
weigh anchor near The Finger. Longboats are rowed from these
ships to the little wooden dock beside Milly's, to pick up or
land passengers, to get fresh water & to unload goods. And of
course sailors & passengers alike always take the opportunity
to sample Milly's chowder & enjoy her company while they are
ashore.

If you wish to visit Blood Lily Island, the closer & smaller
of the 2 islands you can see from The Finger (& the only island
that it is safe to land upon), you can hire a boat from Milly for
a small fee. Be aware that though the strait between the island
& the mainland looks narrow, strong currents & rough seas will
ensure that it will take you at least 2 hours to row the distance.

As Blood Lily Island is a favorite dragon haunt, I am going
to make the trip as soon as I have finished my chowder & these
notes. Pearl has been fed & watered. While I am away she will
enjoy her rest in Milly's stable, sheltered from the everlasting
wind.

Notes for Safe Travel in Diamond Territory

Diamond territory can be dangerous for the traveler who is unprepared. Take note of the following precautions:

❈ Check your supplies of snakebite cure & bandages & renew if necessary.

❈ Ask at the first store, tavern or dwelling you see for Gripper Salve & buy at least 1 jar. Milly's Chowder House charges 1 gold coin for 2 jars. This is good value.

❈ Buy or obtain at least 20 fish heads, chunks of overripe cheese or pieces of strong-smelling sausage. Wrap these items tightly in an oiled cloth to stop the smell from overpowering you & attracting predators. Keep the package with you at all times.

❈ Be extremely polite to everyone you meet, however roughly dressed. Be prepared for the fact that Jalis smell rather strong. This is because they believe that bathing causes weakness. Instead of bathing they rub their skin with melted Tusker fat mixed with strengthening herbs.
  If you offend by mistake & are threatened, apologize at once. Do not draw your weapon. No Jalis will fight an unarmed person in time of peace. Remember that it is far better to be called a coward than to fight a pointless battle you will certainly lose.

❈ If you cannot find lodging in a farmhouse or inn & must sleep outdoors, avoid forest. The best place to camp is beside a sturdy tree in otherwise open ground. It is safe to sleep on sandy shore, as long as you choose a spot above the high tide line.

❈ Read my notes under Dangers of Diamond Territory & follow the advice closely.

Dangers of Diamond Territory

Following are some of the most common natural dangers
of Diamond territory, both in the sea & on land. Some
appear harmless at first sight, which makes them even
more of a threat.

Kobbs

These ferocious creatures have fish-like tails & flippers
instead of forelegs. They live on land but spend much
of their time in the sea. They are always golden-brown
in color & can grow to a vast size in old age. They are
hairless, but have thick "manes" of long, loose streamers
of skin that look like fronds of seaweed.

    A Kobb seeking prey in the sea drifts around very
slowly. The flabby strands of its mane float wide around it,
so it looks like nothing more than a mat of seaweed. Fish,
birds, small sea serpents & any other creatures that stray

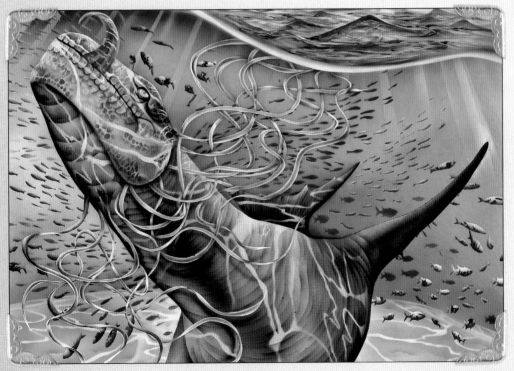

The ferocious Kobb

too close to this harmless-looking mat are snapped up with ease by the Kobb's long, bristly blue tongue. Do not wade, swim or even go out in a boat if you can see what looks like a large seaweed mat drifting nearby.

A Kobb on land is even more dangerous, particularly when it is defending its den from intruders. It moves surprisingly fast, its body protected by the silvery slime that oozes from its skin. The slime trail it leaves hardens to a smooth finish in the sun. If you come upon a coastal place where the rocks shine & are smooth as glass, remove yourself with all speed. You are nearing the den of a Kobb.

Sea Serpents

Most folk are well aware of the dangers of sea serpents, but I mention them here because they have lately become very common in the Ocean of the South, even in quite shallow water. No doubt this is because for years there have been fewer Diamond dragons to take serpents while they are young.

A double dose of snakebite cure, tight bandaging to stop loss of blood & complete rest will go some way toward helping a victim of a mild sea serpent attack. Pain relief is also helpful.

Bird Banes

These transparent, eel-like creatures are as thin as arrows & when adult are about as long as a man's arm. Their small heads seem nothing but staring eyes & hinged jaws full of needle-sharp teeth. They specialize in shooting vertically from the water & snatching birds from the air, but they will attack anything that moves on or above the surface of the sea.

When boating, do not lean over the side of the boat, point or peer over the side or trail your hand in the water. If you do, you will risk Bird Bane attack. Once attached to a victim, a Bird Bane will not release its grip under any circumstances. Even if its head is torn from its body, its jaws will remain locked & the teeth will remain

A Bird Bane takes a victim

embedded in the flesh. The resulting pain, shock & blood loss have caused many human deaths.

Diamond Territory fisherfolk catch Bird Banes by holding thin rods tipped with lumps of wax over the water. They use the attached Bird Banes as live bait to catch larger fish.

Tuskers

Herds of wild pigs roam the hills & plains of Diamond territory, just as packs of wolves roam the north. The Jalis call these pigs "Tuskers." They are far larger & stronger than ordinary pigs & have humped backs. Their thick hides are covered with coarse, bristly hair that is generally gray-brown in color, sometimes spotted with black or white.

They are extremely aggressive & will attack any creature they come across. Both male & female pigs have tusks. The Jalis hunt Tuskers for food & sport, but I would not advise you to attempt it. You are more likely to be eaten than to eat. Besides, Tusker meat is extremely tough & smelly.

Your best defense against Tusker attack is to throw the beasts some of the fish heads, cheese or sausage chunks you are carrying with you. While the pigs are distracted by this strong-smelling food, hasten to climb a tree. The Tuskers will remain below the tree for half an hour or so, bumping the trunk to try to dislodge you, but will at last lose interest & move away.

Diamond Pythons

Diamond Pythons are very large snakes, easily recognized by the distinctive green & yellow diamond pattern on their backs. They have poisonous fangs but usually kill by crushing their prey, which they then swallow whole. They continue to grow throughout their long lives. The largest I have seen measured 20 of my paces from its head to the tip of its tail. I dared to take this measurement only because the python was digesting a Tusker at the time, so was too sleepy to move.

Diamond Pythons have the interesting habit of swallowing smooth stones to help them digest their meals. A stone taken from the belly of a Diamond Python is regarded by the Jalis as a powerful talisman.

Diamond Pythons can climb trees & move very fast despite their size. They are usually found in thickly forested areas. This is why it is unwise to sleep in Diamond territory forests, especially near water.

Grippers

These flesh-eating plants are found throughout Diamond territory, especially in the fields of the south. Their broad, bright green leaves make flat circles on the ground. Their

A Gripper with fangs displayed

small flowers are purple. They spread rapidly, so are usually found in groups.

A Gripper looks like a harmless weed, but if you step on it the leaves will instantly spring apart & your foot will plunge deep into the plant's gaping central "throat." The throat is lined with fangs that point downward, digging deep into the flesh as the Gripper's victim struggles to get free. The fangs also inject a fluid that makes blood flow very freely.

Pain & blood loss will normally cause a Gripper's victim to lose consciousness in a very few minutes. If no one comes to the rescue, the gripper will then slowly drag its victim into the ground for digestion.

Victims of Gripper attack who are saved by companions still often die of blood loss & infection. The usual remedies for injury are of little use. The only way to treat Gripper bite is to smother the wounds with a gray paste the Jalis call "Gripper Salve." You can buy it throughout Diamond territory. All farmhouses keep a good supply. It smells & looks vile, but is effective.

Grippers are so dangerous to beasts & humans alike
& spread so quickly that since the time of Adin troops
of the king's guards have marched from Del to Diamond
territory each year to help the local people weed their
fields of Grippers & keep them under control. I pray this
help will continue.

Blood Lily Island

I am writing this on Blood Lily Island. As I had hoped, I
found a Diamond dragon here, feeding on the flowers that
give the island its name. She welcomed me soberly, for she
is grieving. Her mate was killed by Ak-Baba a few weeks
ago—killed on the ground as he gathered nesting stones
while she was away hunting.

The dragon has now returned to her grazing, but I
can see that she has little heart for food. She eats with
stubborn determination. She is building up her strength.
She is planning to take her revenge on the beasts from the
Shadowlands, or die in the attempt.

I must persuade her not to take the risk. I must tell
her that she has to keep herself safe. The survival of her
tribe is at stake.

Blood Lily Island is linked to its larger neighbor,
the Isle of the Dead, by a natural rock bridge that is
gradually being worn into an arch by the crashing waves.
You can stand on this bridge to get a closer look at the
larger island, if you wish, but stay well back. The Isle of
the Dead is not safe.

Blood Lilies & Fleshbanes

Blood Lily Island is so named because it is the only place
in Deltora where the rare & curious scarlet flowers called
Blood Lilies grow.

Blood Lilies

Fleshbanes

Blood Lilies & Fleshbanes

You will find the Blood Lily patch on the south side of the island. The bright flowers have a sweet scent & abundant nectar, so animals & birds are attracted to them. You may also be tempted to walk among them, but DO NOT DO IT.

Among the lily petals, perfectly disguised by shape & color, lurk red, beetle-like creatures called Fleshbanes.

Blood Lily pollen penetrates hair, feathers, cloth & leather & has a numbing effect when it falls on the skin. The Fleshbanes crawl out of hiding & attach themselves to the numbed areas. Using their razor-sharp pincers they rapidly cut through any protective covering till they reach the flesh. They then eat their fill without their victim's knowledge. Fleshbanes are small, but as they usually attack in large numbers the results can be fatal. If you look carefully at the roots of the Blood Lilies, you will see how well the plants have been fed by the carcasses of birds, animals & humans who have fallen victim to their Fleshbane partners.

Fleshbanes cannot live without Blood Lilies &
fortunately the lilies spread very slowly. Diamond dragons
graze on them occasionally & this has helped to keep their
numbers down as well. The lily patch has hardly increased
in size at all since my first visit to the island many years
ago. If this were not so, Blood Lily Island would be a
dangerous place indeed. As it is, it is a pleasant spot for a
picnic.

The Isle of the Dead

This island is NOT a pleasant spot for a picnic. View it
from the rock bridge, by all means, but do not be tempted
to visit it. At its peak is a cavern that has always been a

Kobb den. This has given the
island its ominous name, for no
one can set foot on its barren
surface without being attacked
and killed. Kobbs have also
given the island its smooth,
shining surface. The slime
produced by generations of the
beasts has made the barren
rocks glassy so that they shine
in the sun.

Over the years, Jalis
knights & dragons alike have
attacked the Isle of the Dead,
seeking to rid it of the Kobbs
that inhabit it. But no sooner
is 1 Kobb killed or driven away
from the island than another
eagerly takes its place.

My opinion is that Kobbs
must live somewhere & that it
does no harm for the Isle of the
Dead to be exclusive to their
use. It is a barren, isolated,

The Isle of the Dead

windswept place surrounded by rough seas that will drive the sturdiest boat onto the rocks. Few Deltorans wish to visit it. Why not leave it to the curious creatures that find it so appealing?

All that matters is that visitors do not stumble onto it unaware of its danger. These notes, I hope, will make the danger of such accidents a little less.

———◆———

Another conversation with the dragon of the Diamond has given me food for thought. To convince her of her tribe's danger, I showed her my sketch of the Toran fortune-telling stones. She pointed a talon at the "trust" symbol beside the "dragon" symbol, snorted & said: "Trust! Now that my mate is dead, there is nothing in this world I trust but the land—& you, Dragonfriend."

I was very moved by her words. It seems that, like the Jalis & the dragon of the Diamond, I hide a tender heart beneath my hard shell.

But my friend's words stayed with me. And I suddenly saw that perhaps I had the power to do something to rescue the last of Deltora's dragons after all.

It would be difficult. I would be taking a risk . . . they would all be taking a risk.

But they trust me. So perhaps it could be done.

———◆———

Jaliad

Pearl & I are now in Jaliad, the city of the Jalis. We traveled here from The Finger by moving east along the Coast Road, then branching off to the left to follow the broad track known as Knight's Parade. The turnoff is clearly marked.

Jaliad does not have many grand buildings & it may seem smelly, dirty & disorganized to travelers fresh from the elegance of Tora, but it is a city of great life and energy. Its people seem rough & are at first suspicious of strangers, but soon warm to those who are agreeable & are clearly enjoying themselves. Just keep my advice under "Notes for Safe Travel in Diamond Territory" in mind & your visit to Jaliad will bring you nothing but pleasure.

Where to Stay?

Try The Diamond, The Knight's Arms or The Jolly Pig. All are taverns with a few upstairs bedrooms. All 3 are noisy & not very clean, but they do supply sheets & pillows—rarities in Jaliad. They are also less likely to be the scenes of brawls than other, cheaper taverns in the town. All provide good stables for horses.

I am staying at The Diamond, where a large bowl of thick chicken & dumpling soup & all the bread you can eat is included in the price of a room. I have spent the day checking that everything in the city is as I remember it. Now I write these notes sitting on my narrow bed (which the room is only just large enough to hold!) by the light of a candle. The floorboards & door are shaking with the din of singing below. It is just as well that I have work to do. It would be hard to sleep.

Things to Do in Jaliad

❧ Visit the central marketplace. It is like a symbol of the city as a whole because it is so busy & noisy. You can restore your food & first-aid supplies here & buy gifts for those you have left at home. The Jalis are not great craftspeople themselves, but they buy & sell all sorts of strange & beautiful objects that are brought to their coast by foreign ships.

In the marketplace you will also find many good-luck charms & talismans for sale, as well as herbal brews and lotions that are supposed to have strengthening powers. The Jalis may be a strong, war-like people, but at heart they are as superstitious as the folk of the Mere.

Jalis knights in training

❦ Beside the marketplace is the arena where the knights
& knights in training exercise & stage mock battles.
Bench seats surround the arena & spectators are welcome,
though strangers to the city must state their names &
allow themselves to be searched by the guards at the
gates before entering. There is no limit on the number of
weapons a visitor can carry into the arena, but concealed
weapons are forbidden. All weapons must be clearly
visible.

❦ The great feasting hall on the other side of the market
square is where Jalis knights & commoners meet to eat,
sing & hear old tales told. It is easy to gain an invitation
to eat in the hall. Merely ask the guard at the door &
offer a gold coin as payment for your meal. (Do not offer
silver. This would be regarded as an insult.) Your coin will
be refused, but it must be offered to show that you value
the honor you are about to receive.
    Once your eyes have become accustomed to the
smoke & dimness in the hall you will see long tables
with benches on either side of them. Find a place &

help yourself from the nearest platter. The food usually consists of fruit, roast pumpkin, hard Jalis bread & meat cut in chunks from the whole beasts turning on spits at the end of the room. The meat may be too bloody for your taste, but on no account show disgust.

Do not refuse the beaker of ale that will be given to you. The Jalis do not trust folk who will not drink with them. But be cautious—Jalis ale is very strong.

You will be expected to eat with your knife & your fingers. It is usual to throw bones onto the floor when they have been picked clean. It is usual to belch loudly at the end of the meal, as a sign that you have eaten well.

If you are lucky, you will be in the feasting hall when Ruff, the present Jalis storyteller, tells a tale. Ruff's voice seems to have the power to entrance his audience & the stories he tells, generally the ancient fables called "The Tenna Birdsong Tales,"* are fascinating no matter how many times they are heard.

*The Tenna Birdsong Tales

It is said that these traditional Jalis folktales were first told in ancient days to Tenna, a young Jalis girl, by a blackbird she had released from a net.

Strangers to Diamond territory are sometimes surprised to find that the practical Jalis do not doubt this story, but believe it wholeheartedly. In my opinion, there is no reason why the story should not be true. The blackbirds of Deltora are highly intelligent & I have seen them communicate with humans with whom they have bonded.

The Tenna Birdsong Tales have been passed down from generation to generation of Jalis storytellers and are always told in the same words. When the 7 tribes were united, Adin caused them to be written down in the *Deltora Annals* (Volume 1). They make interesting reading, not only because they are entertaining but also because, despite their fanciful language, they are based on grains of truth & trace our ancient history. The dragons have assured me that this is so.

Main Roads from Jaliad

❧ Jaliad Road runs through the center of the city &
continues east until it reaches Deltora Way. Turn right at
Deltora Way to return to Del.

Note: Beware of bandits near the Topaz border & keep
watch for Tuskers crossing your path.

❧ Knight's Parade, the road I used to reach Jaliad from The
Finger, runs right through the city & continues north. It is
the road to take for all the northern territories. At the point
where the borders of Diamond, Lapis Lazuli & Amethyst
territories meet, Knight's Parade becomes a narrower track
called Wander Road. Follow this till you reach Deltora
Way, then turn left for Tora & Emerald territory, right for
Rithmere & Hira.

❧ Greel's Trail is named for the famous Jalis leader who first
pledged loyalty to Adin. This road runs southeast from Jaliad
all the way to the Coast Road near the Topaz border. It makes
for rougher traveling, because of the hills it climbs, but it is
a useful shortcut. Another advantage of using Greel's Trail
is the wild & beautiful countryside through which you will
travel. The glorious valley of Haven Vale, teeming with bird
& animal life, is an outstanding example.

During the past few days I have thought carefully about
the idea that occurred to me on Blood Lily Island. I have a
plan now & I am determined to try to carry it out. I will be
leaving Jaliad tomorrow at first light, following Greel's Trail
to the Coast Road. I will travel as fast as Pearl is able until I
cross the Topaz border & reach my last stopping point before
my return to Del—Withick Mire.

My long, hard journey has taken me through wondrous
places in all of Deltora's 7 territories. My garments are
wearing very, very thin, the good old leather belt is badly
cracked & I smell of dragons. At Withick I will soon begin to
feel better & bless its peace, the calm presence of a friend &
birdsong when I wake.

13.

Withick Mire

Blazing words
Burn three dragons last.

Traditional Topaz dragon saying

*P*earl & I have arrived in Withick Mire, which is not far from Del. It is a swampy place, richly green, where wild orchids hang from the trees like bats & strange lights dance in the mists that rise over the waters at dusk. Once it was simply called "the Mire," but over the years it has come to be known by the name of the famous man who has made it his home.

Withick is an old friend of mine. He lives alone here. He was glad to see me, give me a bed & listen to my plans.

If you have read my notes on the palace in Del you will know that Withick is a genius of many talents. You will also know that it was Withick who painted the scenes from Deltora's past on the ceilings of the great rooms of the palace.

He left the palace & retired to the peace of the Mire after Chief Advisor Drumm objected to a book Withick had written & printed when his paintings had been completed.

Withick was inspired to produce the book as a result of his study of Deltora's oldest stories for his painting work. He called the book simply *The Belt of Deltora*. It told of the Belt's history, magic & power. The book was small & was not decorated in any way, for Withick said he wanted nothing to distract the reader from the words.

Drumm said it was impertinent for a commoner like Withick to write about the Belt of Deltora, which was the business of the king alone. He said Withick had become swollen with ridiculous ideas of his own importance. He said the book was an insult to the king, because it had no illustrations & was plainly bound in blue. He gathered up all the copies he could find and had them burned. Withick left the palace in protest & never returned.

He is a very old man now, but his fame has continued to grow & spread. He is now regarded as Deltora's most important artist & the few paintings he produces each year are bought for enormous sums. I met him years ago when I was very young & he was already living in the Mire. Despite the difference in our ages, we became firm friends. We think alike.

I have been able to help Withick in various ways over the years & now he is helping me.

I have decided to give Chief Advisor Drumm a surprise. Instead of the rough manuscript he expects, he will receive a finished masterpiece, printed & illustrated by the famous Withick. The book will be of such great value that while it may be copied, it can never be tampered with. Prince Gareth will receive it intact.

Withick would have preferred to copy the book afresh. He dislikes erasing my original notes. He says my writing & sketches, with all their additions & crossings out, should be preserved because they will be of interest to future scholars. I think this unlikely, but in any case it cannot be helped. As I told Withick, some things are more important than others.

Withick copied everything, therefore, except those few notes I had written on odd scraps of paper when I did not have the official book with me. He insisted on merely pasting these in place, saying that they, at least, were original.

I will have to stay in Withick Mire for some weeks while Withick completes his work. I regret this, but it cannot be helped. At least it means that Pearl will have a long rest. This is good, because once the book is safely delivered to the palace, we must set out at once on a new journey to try to save the last of Deltora's dragons. The water I took from the Dreaming Spring will allow me to locate the 7 quickly. I only pray they remain safe until I can be with them again.

May the spirit of the great Adin strengthen me. May the dragons' trust in me prove stronger than their distrust of each other. And may my memories comfort me in the loneliness to come. Whatever may happen to me in the future, I am glad I have written this book. I have lived a solitary life, but there are things I know about Deltora that no one else can know. It would be a pity to tell no one.

May my memories comfort me in the loneliness to come . . .

A palace library corner . . .

Afterword

Doran the Dragonlover thought that by using the famous artist Withick to copy and illustrate his book he would ensure that it would reach Prince Gareth's hands uncensored and intact. Sadly, he did not count on King Lucan being so gravely ill on his return. Neither did he count on the ruthlessness and cleverness of Drumm, Lucan's traitorous chief advisor.

Drumm would not have wanted Gareth to read the many controversial remarks that Doran could not resist including in his text—especially his passionate defense of dragons, the protectors of the land. It seems that Drumm simply told the king and the court that a book illuminated by Withick was too valuable to be handled—especially by a boy as young as Gareth, who was only fifteen years old at the time.

Lucan was in no position to object. For months he had been ravaged by a mysterious illness that sapped his strength. According to the *Deltora Annals* the palace doctors had tried every way they knew to cure him, without success. This is not surprising, since we can be fairly sure that he was being slowly poisoned by Drumm.

So the precious book on which Doran had pinned all his hopes was locked away in a display case & Prince Gareth, for whom it was intended, probably never even knew it existed. He certainly never read it. If he had, the future of Deltora (and my own life) might have been very different.

Because he did not read Doran's book, Gareth never read Withick's little volume, *The Belt of Deltora*, either. Doran had tried to ensure that he did. Look at the white glow in the illustration of the palace library corner: I am certain that this was where one of the last surviving copies of *The Belt of Deltora* was hidden. Doran and Withick had probably decided to place it there in the hope that Gareth would find it.

Gareth never did, but it was found centuries later by someone else, who understood its main message: that the great Adin, understanding the Shadow Lord's wicked patience, endless plans and burning will to conquer Deltora at last, wore the Belt always and never let it out of his sight.

No wonder Drumm suppressed the little blue book, destroying all copies he could find. As a servant of the Shadow Lord, his duty was to keep the Belt and Adin's heir apart.

The fact that Doran's book was not itself "accidentally" destroyed makes me sure that, as Doran had hoped, Drumm failed to understand the hints in the last two paragraphs of the Author's Note, or find the "important message" for Prince Gareth that Doran had buried deep within his manuscript.

The important message is a letter, made up from secret sentences hidden in every chapter. Doran's Note gives a small clue on how to find them. If you want more help, there is a hint printed upside down at the bottom of the next page.

It seems only fair to give this to you. The instructions on how to read the hidden messages are given in a code that Doran must have taught Gareth when Gareth was a child. It is a code I learned myself not so many years ago. Perhaps if I had not known it, I would not have found the secret messages, either!

Doran never knew that his book had been suppressed.
After delivering it, he resumed his travels, determined
to carry out his plan to save Deltora's last dragons by
persuading them to sleep until the skies were safe again.
Rumors that he was losing his mind were already circulating
in the palace at this time, so his warnings before leaving
were ignored. He learned too much and spoke too much
and within a year he had disappeared, a victim of Shadow
Lord evil.

Soon after Doran's delivery of his book and departure
from Del, Withick the artist was found dead in his hut in
Withick Mire. How he died is unclear, though we may draw
our own grim conclusions. His death brought Drumm and
Drumm's master in the Shadowlands two great benefits.
One, it ensured that Doran's book became even more
priceless and untouchable than before. And two, there was
no one left to alert Prince Gareth to what Doran had been
trying to tell him.

Doran's plan that Prince Gareth would wake the sleeping
dragons failed. More time had to pass before the dragons
awoke than he would ever have dreamed. But in the end
a young king did put on the Belt of Deltora, banish the
Ak-Baba and wake Deltora's sleeping protectors. Today
dragons once again ride the wind over Deltoran skies.

I like to think that the spirit of Doran flies with them.

Lief of Del

A hint for reading Doran's secret messages: the lines of "dragon poetry" at the beginning of each
chapter are nonsense. Take out all words that could concern dragons or fire & read the remaining
words backward. Follow the instructions given to find the secret sentences in each chapter.

No part of this publication may be reproduced, stored in a retrieval system, or transmitted in
any form or by any means, electronic, mechanical, photocopying, recording, or otherwise, without
written permission of the publisher. For information regarding permission, write to Permissions
Department, Scholastic Australia, PO Box 579, Lindfield, New South Wales, Australia 2070.

ISBN-13: 978-0-545-06933-5
ISBN-10: 0-545-06933-5

First published by Scholastic Australia in 2008.
Text copyright © Emily Rodda, 2008.
Deltora Quest concept and characters copyright © Emily Rodda.
Deltora Quest is a registered trademark of Rin Pty Ltd.
Illustrations copyright © Scholastic Australia Pty Ltd., 2008.
Illustrations by Marc McBride.

All rights reserved. Published by Scholastic Inc. SCHOLASTIC and associated logos are
trademarks and/or registered trademarks of Scholastic Inc.

12   11   10   9   8   7   6   5   4   3   2   1   9   10   11   12   13   14/0

Printed in China

First American edition, October 2009